DANGER IN THE SNOW

Frank and Joe found themselves back in the canyon where they had met K. D. Becker and the hungry mountain lion.

"Looks like she spent the night here," Frank observed, nodding toward a red backpack that was propped up against a pine tree.

Joe's ski scraped against something buried in the snow. Brushing away the snow, he uncovered a long cylinder with a tiny antenna attached. "Maybe she was looking for this," he said.

"I don't think she's looking for anything anymore," Frank said grimly. His eyes were fixed on something beyond the red backpack, on the far side of the pine tree. It was another splash of red, but this one was darker and round.

Under the blood-soaked patch of snow, deathly still, lay K. D. Becker.

Books in THE HARDY BOYS CASEFILES™ Series

#1 DEAD ON TARGET
#2 EVIL, INC.
#3 CULT OF CRIME
#4 THE LAZARUS PLOT
#5 EDGE OF DESTRUCTION
#6 THE CROWNING TERROR
#7 DEATHGAME
#8 SEE NO EVIL
#9 THE GENIUS THIEVES
#10 HOSTAGES OF HATE
#11 BROTHER AGAINST BROTHER
#12 PERFECT GETAWAY
#13 THE BORGIA DAGGER
#14 TOO MANY TRAITORS
#15 BLOOD RELATIONS
#16 LINE OF FIRE
#17 THE NUMBER FILE
#18 A KILLING IN THE MARKET
#19 NIGHTMARE IN ANGEL CITY
#20 WITNESS TO MURDER
#21 STREET SPIES
#22 DOUBLE EXPOSURE
#23 DISASTER FOR HIRE
#24 SCENE OF THE CRIME
#25 THE BORDERLINE CASE
#26 TROUBLE IN THE PIPELINE
#27 NOWHERE TO RUN
#28 COUNTDOWN TO TERROR
#29 THICK AS THIEVES
#30 THE DEADLIEST DARE
#31 WITHOUT A TRACE
#32 BLOOD MONEY
#33 COLLISION COURSE
#34 FINAL CUT
#35 THE DEAD SEASON
#36 RUNNING ON EMPTY
#37 DANGER ZONE
#38 DIPLOMATIC DECEIT
#39 FLESH AND BLOOD
#40 FRIGHT WAVE
#41 HIGHWAY ROBBERY
#42 THE LAST LAUGH
#43 STRATEGIC MOVES
#44 CASTLE FEAR
#45 IN SELF-DEFENSE
#46 FOUL PLAY
#47 FLIGHT INTO DANGER
#48 ROCK 'N' REVENGE
#49 DIRTY DEEDS
#50 POWER PLAY
#51 CHOKE HOLD
#52 UNCIVIL WAR
#53 WEB OF HORROR
#54 DEEP TROUBLE
#55 BEYOND THE LAW
#56 HEIGHT OF DANGER
#57 TERROR ON TRACK
#58 SPIKED!
#59 OPEN SEASON

Available from ARCHWAY Paperbacks

OPEN SEASON

FRANKLIN W. DIXON

AN ARCHWAY PAPERBACK
Published by POCKET BOOKS
New York London Toronto Sydney Tokyo Singapore

This book is a work of fiction. Names, characters, places, and incidents are either the product of the author's imagination or are used fictitiously. Any resemblance to actual events or locales or persons, living or dead, is entirely coincidental.

AN ARCHWAY PAPERBACK *Original*

An Archway Paperback published by
POCKET BOOKS, a division of Simon & Schuster Inc.
1230 Avenue of the Americas, New York, NY 10020

Produced by Mega-Books of New York, Inc.

ISBN: 0-671-73095-9

First Archway Paperback printing January 1992

10 9 8 7 6 5 4 3 2 1

Cover art by Brian Kotzky

Printed in the U.S.A.

OPEN SEASON

Chapter 1

"IF THIS IS A TRAIL," Joe Hardy said, stopping next to his brother, "I'm a grizzly bear. I can't see anything but snow."

Frank Hardy slipped his sunglasses up on top of his head. "It would be kind of hard to get around on cross-country skis *without* snow." He cast a glance at his brother. "And I don't think a bear would be caught dead in that electric blue body suit."

Joe looked at his tight-fitting, one-piece, insulated ski suit. "Hey, this is the cutting edge of ski technology and fashion. It's lightweight, gives me room to move—and it matches my baby blues."

Frank chuckled. "Right. And the neon yellow ski cap matches your hair. But I know what you mean about wanting everything to be as light as possible," he said, shifting his shoulders. "These backpacks are heavy."

Frank's outfit consisted of a dark gray wool sweater and hat and loose-fitting, insulated black nylon ski pants. Underneath it all, he wore synthetic thermal underwear from neck to ankle. The dark colors would absorb the sun's heat better than light ones, but Joe's flashy suit would protect him from the cold just as well. Their choice of clothes simply reflected the difference in their personalities.

With his sunglasses pulled down, Joe scanned the mountain peaks in the distance, ready to kick off again. "We sure have come a long way from Bayport," he said. "It's hard to believe we were on the East Coast yesterday, and now we're in the middle of nowhere."

"I don't think the good citizens of Colorado consider the Rocky Mountains nowhere," Frank replied.

"What citizens?" Joe asked. "We're about eight miles from the nearest town and three miles from the trailhead where we left our rented car. We won't see another human being for the next three days."

"That's the whole point of this trip," Frank said. "No crowds, no noise, nothing between us and nature."

"Nothing except several layers of clothes," Joe pointed out.

"Sorry you came?" Frank asked.

Joe planted his pole behind him and turned to study the terrain. They were halfway down a gentle slope into a valley dotted with pine trees. The sky was the deepest blue Joe had ever seen. The clear air made all colors seem richer and purer, even the blanket of white snow. Every breath he took of the crisp mountain air made him feel more alive.

"Not a bit," he finally said.

Frank smiled, sensing what his brother was feeling.

Joe pushed off with his poles and got back into the kick-and-glide rhythm of cross-country skiing. "Come on!" he shouted with his typical impatient enthusiasm. "Let's see how many miles we can cover today!"

Frank aimed his skis into the twin grooves carved by his brother in front of him. Even though Frank, at eighteen, was a year older, it was usually easier to let Joe lead. In back-country skiing, a broad outline of a trail was mapped out, but each person was left to pick out a specific path over the steep, rolling terrain. This demanded a lot more from a skier than cruising along on well-worn, packed, and groomed paths. So Frank was content to let Joe do the hard work for a while.

Joe wasn't a machine, though, and Frank had no intention of letting him push himself until he collapsed from exhaustion. "Ease up a bit," he called out. "We're not in a hurry to get anywhere, and we're not used to this altitude. The air's a lot thinner here than back home. Just relax and enjoy the scenery. We've got a whole week of vacation left."

"Yeah," Joe called back. "And that means Christmas break is half over. Eight short days from now we'll be cooped up in a classroom at Bayport High again. I want to see everything there is to see in this national forest before then."

Frank laughed. "In that case, we're doing it the wrong way. If you want to cover the entire Gunnison National Forest, you should have rented a plane."

They were soon on the other side of the small valley, and the trail sloped upward again, slowing Joe down a little. "These new waxless skis Dad gave us for Christmas are great," he said. "Plenty of grip when you need it going uphill, and they don't seem to cut down on the glide. I could keep up this pace all day."

"That's what *you* think," Frank said as they reached the top of the ridge. "Let's stop here for a short rest, anyway. We need to put some fuel into our systems."

"If you mean it's time to eat," Joe replied, "you could easily talk me into that." He didn't like to admit that he was a little tired but could easily confess to being hungry. Just about everything Joe did made him hungry. It wasn't a problem, though, because everything he ate seemed to turn to muscle. At just about six feet, Joe had the body of a serious athlete. But the only thing Joe was ever really serious about for longer than a few days was detective work.

Their passion for solving crimes was one of the few traits the brothers shared and something they inherited from their father. Fenton Hardy was a former New York City detective and was now a successful, internationally known private investigator. Even though Frank and Joe were still in high school, they had cracked plenty of cases already.

Joe slipped out of his skis and jammed the tails into the deep snow so they stood upright. He joined his brother on a rock outcropping at the very crest of the ridge and dug a granola bar out of his backpack. As he munched, he studied the view. It surprised him. It had been a short, easy climb up from the valley, but on the other side, the ground dropped away sharply into a deep gorge.

"We *might* be able to ski down," Joe remarked with some doubt. "It'll be a little rough getting up the other side."

Frank's pack was leaning against a tree. He reached over, unzipped a side pocket, and took out a map of the national forest. "We don't have to worry about it," he said. "The trail follows the top of this ridge for a way."

Joe leaned over and peeked at the map. "Can you tell how high up we are from this thing?" he asked.

"Not exactly," Frank answered. "It's not a detailed terrain map. Some elevations are marked, so maybe I could make a fairly good guess."

"Never mind the guesswork," Joe said. "Where's that gizmo that tells you everything—except how to meet girls? The monocle or moniker—whatever you call it?"

"The monocular," Frank said, pulling a palm-size object out of his pack. It was a compact, lightweight telescope. It was also a lot more: a rangefinder, compass, clock, and altimeter. Frank held it up to his eye and pressed a button on the top. A digital display winked on at the bottom of the circular view of the magnified countryside. "If this thing is accurate, we're at about eighty-one hundred feet."

Joe let out a long, low whistle. "That's over a mile and a half straight up!"

"Well, yes and no," Frank said. "The altimeter measures elevation from sea level, but we didn't start out at the sea."

"Sure we did," Joe countered. "Bayport's at sea level."

Frank shot a look at his brother. "I mean *today*, from the trailhead where we left the car. We were at about seven thousand, seven hundred feet. So even though we've gone about three miles, we've covered only three hundred vertical feet."

"Let me take a look," Joe said.

"Don't believe me?" Frank asked.

"Sure I do," Joe replied. "Three hundred feet uphill in the snow on skis is pretty good, if you ask me. I just want to check out the view."

Frank handed the gadget to his brother, and Joe peered down into the gorge. He followed the winding path of what was probably a frozen stream.

"What are you looking for?" Frank asked after a few minutes.

"I don't know," Joe said, sounding slightly disappointed. "An elk or a deer or something. What's the point of being out in the wild if you don't see any wildlife?" Just then he caught a glimpse of movement in the distance.

"Hang on, there's something down there." He spotted it again. This time there was more than one "something" moving.

Joe handed the monocular back to Frank and pointed. "Remember what I said about not seeing another human being for the next three days? I was wrong."

Frank studied the scene through the telescopic lens. At first he didn't see anything but trees, snow, and rocks. Then he saw it: a bright orange shape moving slowly across an open patch of snow. Three more brightly colored shapes came into view moving up the gorge, and the glint of metal flashed in the midday sun. At least two of the figures were carrying rifles.

"Hunters," he concluded. "They're probably after bighorn sheep."

"Let's hope they don't mistake us for a couple of rams," Joe said.

Frank took another look at his brother's bright blue ski suit. "I don't think you have much to worry about."

Joe jumped to his feet. "Right, but let's put some distance between us and them, anyway." He eyed the subdued earth tones of his brother's outfit. "Maybe you should wear this," he added, holding out his neon yellow ski cap.

"Good idea," Frank said, trading hats with his brother. "This is almost as good as one of those orange safety vests."

The Hardys didn't see the hunters again and quickly forgot about them. It was a beautiful day, and they were surrounded by spectacular scenery. A few hours after they left the ridge, the trail led them into a narrow canyon. Frank was leading the way, for a change, when he stopped suddenly. Joe almost crashed into him.

"Time for another snack break?" Joe asked hopefully.

"Maybe," Frank replied slowly. "I guess it depends on who's doing the snacking."

Then Joe noticed what had stopped his brother cold. "Wow. Are those what I think they are?"

Frank nodded. "Mountain lion tracks. Judging from the size of the prints, it's a pretty big cat." He stooped down to take a closer look. "The edges are a bit blurred. They don't look too fresh. They might be from yesterday or even the day before. This canyon is pretty well sheltered from the wind."

"It's probably long gone," Joe said, scanning the immediate area. A mound of snow by the canyon wall caught his eye. "It looks like he left his calling card, though."

Frank followed to where his brother was pointing to something sticking out of the snow. It appeared to be a frozen animal hoof. "Well, there's that elk you wanted to see," he said grimly. "But I don't think there'll be much to look at now."

"Let's check it out, anyway," Joe said, already gliding toward the half-buried carcass. He wasn't really interested in a dead elk but was very curious about the habits of one of the last big predators still roaming free in North America.

"I don't think that's a good idea," Frank started to say.

Too late, Joe realized that his brother was right. A hissing growl made him freeze in his tracks. He lifted his head slowly and stared up into the snarling fangs of a cougar perched on the ledge above him. Its tan fur blended in perfectly with the surrounding rocks. The mountain lion was crouched low on the rock, every muscle taut, ready to spring.

Joe could see his own pale image in the cat's cold, yellow eyes. There was no compassion in those eyes—only the hunger of a deadly hunter.

Chapter 2

JOE KNEW IT WAS useless to try to make a run for it—the big cat could bring him down and tear him to pieces in seconds.

The cougar bared its fangs and snarled again. Joe slowly lowered one ski pole to the ground and clutched the other with both hands. The fiberglass shaft with the steel tip was his only weapon. Joe Hardy wouldn't go down without a fight.

Suddenly a sharp crack rang out. The cat shrieked and leapt high in the air. Joe ducked, thrusting the ski pole up and out in front of him. He braced for the impact of several hundred pounds of fur and teeth and claws.

It never came. The cougar didn't touch him. After it jumped straight up, it thumped right back down on the ledge, whirling around and swatting at its flank as if it had been stung by a bee.

Joe saw doubt and confusion in the big cat's eyes now. The cougar paced nervously across the ledge. Then, all of a sudden, its back legs buckled. It snapped its head around, surprised that half its body had decided to take a nap. Its front legs gave way next, and the cat slumped down on the rock. It gave one last, halfhearted hiss. Its eyes closed slowly, and the mighty predator forgot about having Joe for lunch.

Joe stood up warily, not sure what had happened. A camouflage-clad figure, gripping a high-powered rifle, dropped out of a nearby pine. "Nobody move!" a commanding voice ordered through a dark ski mask. The stranger who had just saved Joe's life stomped toward him, thrust the rifle at him, and gruffly said, "Here, hold this."

The ski mask came off—and the hunter shook out her long brown hair. "I've been sitting in that tree for eight hours, waiting for that cat to come back. Then you two come along and almost blow it."

Joe was too stunned to say anything. First, he was almost cougar chow. Now he was being scolded by an angry female hunter.

The woman gave him a sharp look. "What are you doing with that rifle? Don't point it at the ground. Keep it trained on the cat. If he starts to move, put another round into his flank." She turned and started to trudge back toward her pine tree.

"Hey, wait a minute," Joe called. "I'm not going to kill that mountain lion for you!"

"You'd better not!" she shouted back. "I've spent the last decade trying to keep him alive!"

Frank wandered over for a closer look and nudged his brother. "Notice anything strange about that cougar?"

That was when Joe spotted the dart sticking in the cat's side and the thick black collar around its neck.

"She hit him with a tranquilizer dart," Frank said. "He's out cold, but when the drug wears off, he'll be fine."

Joe pointed at a short metal strand poking out of a boxy bulge in the cat's collar. "That looks like some kind of antenna."

"Very good," the woman remarked. "For a couple of smart guys, you sure do some dumb things."

Frank hadn't even heard her come up behind them. His attention had been focused on the mountain lion. "I'll admit that my brother doesn't always use the best judgment," he said evenly. "But why did you let him walk right into this situation? You could have warned us."

"The cat had just come back," she answered. "I didn't want to scare him off. I was hoping you'd ski right on by. I guess my judgment's not all that great sometimes, either. Sorry you got caught in the middle of my research." She stuck out her hand. "I'm K. D. Becker."

Frank and Joe both shook hands with her, Frank supplying the introductions.

Becker set down the red backpack that was slung over her shoulder. Frank noticed a two-foot-long, arrow-shaped antenna and a blue metal box lashed to the back of the pack. There was a signal meter set into the top of the box. A socket in the side held an electric cable that led to the antenna.

"I'll bet you knew that cat was coming long before he climbed down the canyon wall," Frank said, nodding toward the blue box. "There's a radio in the cougar's collar, right? You were tracking him with electronic equipment."

"I knew he was heading this way," Becker admitted, "but I didn't know how close he was. It's not a very sophisticated setup."

Joe stooped down to examine the radio telemetry gear. "How does it work?"

"It's a directional antenna," she explained. "You aim it around until you get a signal. Then you head off in that direction and hope you find something."

Frank nodded. "The higher the meter needle jumps, the closer you are."

Becker stared at Frank curiously. "You seem to know a lot about my business."

"Not really," Frank replied. "I don't even

know what your business is. I know something about electronics, that's all."

Frank studied the woman for a moment. She had a long, lean face that suggested a slim body under the bulky clothes. There were a few lines on her face, mostly around her alert green eyes, which told Frank more about her outdoor life than about her age. If he had to guess, he'd say she was in her early thirties, even though she looked younger.

"What did you mean when you said you spent the last decade trying to keep that mountain lion alive?"

"Not just that one," Becker said. "All the cougars in these mountains. The world's closing in on them. We keep carving up the wilderness for towns and resorts. Whatever's left we turn into cattle ranches and mines. A single mountain lion needs thirty or forty square miles for a hunting range. We're running out of space, and the big cats are going to be the losers."

Joe glanced over at the dead elk. "I don't think the other animals would share your concern."

"Mountain lions keep herds healthy," Becker replied. "They hunt the old and the sick, like this one. The cat made the kill about two days ago. He ate all he could and then covered up the rest for later. I knew he'd be back, so I just sat in the tree and waited."

Joe raised his head to eye the slumbering predator. "Now that you've got him, what are you going to do with him?"

"Give him a quick checkup and change the battery in his collar."

"How long do the batteries last?" Frank asked.

"They're *supposed* to be good for at least a year," Becker answered. "Lately some of them have fizzled out after a few months. I've lost track of three cats in the last six weeks. I must have gotten a defective batch of batteries, so I'm trying to replace them all.

"I should be in Washington right now," she continued, "pestering senators and convincing the Fish and Wildlife Service to extend my research grant, but I decided that this is more important."

She walked over to the canyon wall. "It's also fairly important to do it *before* he wakes up." She glanced back at the Hardys. "Could you help me get him down? It'll be a lot easier for me to do my work on the ground."

"No problem," Joe volunteered.

The lip of the ledge was just out of reach. Frank gave Joe a boost, and Joe scrambled up to the cat. Following Becker's instructions, they managed to grapple the cougar down. It was a lot harder than Joe had expected.

"This overgrown kitten must weigh close to two hundred pounds," he groaned as they carefully set the big cat on the ground.

"He tipped the scale at one hundred seventy-nine back in September," Becker said. "He's the biggest cat I've collared." She crouched down, pushed up the cougar's lip, and looked at its teeth.

"How many cats are you tracking?" Frank asked.

"Listen," she replied as she pulled a stethoscope out of her pack, "I love to talk about my work, *except* when I'm working. I also don't want to have to worry about you when my furry friend wakes up. That'll be in about thirty minutes."

She paused. "I'm grateful for your help, but I'd feel a lot better if you were away from here when he wakes up."

"Sounds good to me," Joe said. He wasn't eager for a rematch with the cat. "Will you be okay?"

Becker chuckled. "I've had a lot of practice. I can manage."

With some reluctance, Frank and Joe left K. D. Becker in the canyon with the mountain lion. They skied for an hour and a half more, until dark storm clouds started to push toward them over the mountain peaks in the north. Frank picked out a campsite halfway up a gently sloping hill, where they would be sheltered from the rising wind. They pitched their lightweight dome tent, made a simple dinner on a tiny butane stove, and jumped into their sleeping bags soon after the sun set.

After all the fresh air and exercise, they were soon asleep. Joe was startled awake several times during the night by howling winds buffeting the thin tent walls. At least, he *hoped* it was the wind.

By dawn the tent was half-buried in new snow. It wasn't a problem—in fact, it helped insulate the tent, making it warmer inside. The Hardys ate a breakfast of high-protein granola bars while they waited out the storm. The snow let up once for about fifteen minutes at 9:05, but the sun didn't really come out until a little before ten.

"So where does the trail go from here?" Joe asked as they rolled up the tent.

Frank checked out the trees, their branches sagging under the weight of the new snow. "I think it's time to head back."

Joe stared at him. "What do you mean? We've got enough food and supplies for five days."

"This is avalanche country," Frank explained. "There has been a lot of snow recently, and that big storm last night didn't help the situation. If we keep going, we might get in over our heads—literally."

Joe shrugged his shoulders. "It's your call. This whole trip was your idea, anyway. If we hurry, maybe we can catch a movie tonight. If they have a movie theater in that one-horse town." He paused for a second. "What was it called? Elk Grove?"

"Elk Springs," Frank said.

Joe smiled. "Yeah, that's it. Let's find out if there's anything to do up here that doesn't involve fur and big teeth."

It was late morning when they found themselves back in the canyon where they had met K. D. Becker and the hungry mountain lion.

"Looks like she spent the night here," Frank observed, nodding toward a small mound of white. Peeking out from under the half-inch accumulation was K.D.'s red backpack, propped up against a pine tree.

Joe's ski scraped against something buried in the snow. He glanced down and caught a glimpse of bare metal. Curious, he stopped and prodded it. Brushing away the snow, he uncovered a six-inch-long cylinder with a tiny antenna attached. Joe was surprised by how heavy it was.

"Maybe she was looking for this," he said.

"I don't think she's looking for anything anymore," Frank said grimly. His eyes were fixed on something beyond the red backpack, on the far side of the pine tree. It was another splash of red, but this one was darker and round. Under the blood-soaked patch of snow, deathly still, lay K. D. Becker.

Chapter 3

FRANK AND JOE rushed over to the motionless body. K.D. was flat on her back, her face to the side. A blanket of white covered her except for her chest, which was blood red.

Frank took off his skis and knelt down beside the woman. He put two fingers against the side of her neck and felt a weak pulse. "She's still alive," he told Joe. "If we can get her to a hospital, she may have a chance."

"We should never have left her alone with that cat," Joe said bitterly.

Frank probed the woman's chest gently, feeling for the wound. What he found stunned him. "No mountain lion did this, unless they've got secrets even Becker doesn't know about."

"What do you mean?" Joe asked.

Frank raised his eyes to his brother's. "She's been shot."

"Shot?" Joe echoed. "Why would anyone shoot her?"

"We'll worry about that later," Frank said. "Right now we've got to rig something to carry her on."

"Do you think it's a good idea to move her?" Joe asked, remembering his first-aid training.

"We don't have a choice," Frank replied.

"I could stay with her while you go for help," Joe suggested.

Frank shook his head. "That's three trips instead of one. I'd have to go all the way to Elk Springs to get a doctor or a paramedic, bring the person back here, and then we'd still have to get Becker to a hospital. I don't think she'd last that long, even if the return trips were by chopper.

"But we are in luck," Frank continued. "She got here the same way we did—on cross-country skis."

Joe gave him a blank look. "So what? I don't think she can ski her way out of this."

"Maybe she can," Frank responded while bandaging her wound. "With a little help from us. We can improvise a rescue toboggan from her skis and poles. We'll lash tree branches to the skis across the tips, tails, and bindings to keep the skis about two feet apart. Then we'll lash her poles diagonally to make the whole frame rigid and stronger. To protect her we'll pad the sled with pine boughs and wrap her in her sleeping bag and tent."

"There's just one problem—we have only one rope," Joe said.

"We'll tie it to the skis through the little holes in the tips and drag the sled behind us. For the lashings we'll use any drawstrings in our clothes or packs."

"All right. Let's do it," Joe quickly agreed. He peeled off his ski gloves and stuffed them in his pockets. His hand touched cold metal and came out holding the small cylinder he had found in the snow. "I think this is one of her transmitters," he said, showing the object to his brother.

"Stick it in her pack," Frank said, breaking branches off pines.

Working furiously, they rigged up a pretty stable ski-stretcher. Heading out of the canyon, dragging K.D. behind them, Frank and Joe were soon in a sweat from the long and frustrating haul.

It was afternoon when they finally reached the small, nearly deserted parking lot at the trailhead. They laid Becker in the backseat of their rented sedan, and Frank held her secure while Joe cajoled the car through the fresh layer of snow.

The five-mile trip to Elk Springs took almost an hour on the slippery mountain road. Joe managed to find a way around the worst of the snowdrifts, narrowly avoiding spinning out of control on an icy curve, and breathed a heavy sigh of relief when he saw a blue sign with a large white *H* on it.

"We're in luck," he said. "There's a hospital in this town."

Frank felt Becker's pulse—it was barely more than a flutter now. "We need a little more luck. We're not there yet."

Joe followed the blue signs to a county hospital that was newer and larger than he would have expected. The emergency room doctor took one look at Becker's chest wound and whisked her off to surgery.

The Hardys then had to tackle the questions posed by a stern admitting nurse. Who were they? When was Becker shot? How did it happen? Frank and Joe ran out of useful answers after the first one.

They spent the next hour in the waiting room until the surgeon came out and gave them the news. Becker was alive, but only barely. She was in a coma, and the doctor couldn't say when, or if, she'd come out of it.

"We've got to find the police station and report this," Frank said after the doctor had left.

"You don't have to," a burly man with a droopy mustache drawled. He had been sitting with them in the waiting room, but the Hardys hadn't paid much attention to him. There were streaks of gray in his mustache and hair, at least in the hair that wasn't covered by his Stetson. He was dressed like a rancher—bulky down vest, checked shirt, faded jeans, and work boots.

"Who are you?" Frank asked.

The man tipped back his hat and stood up casually. "I'm Bruce Stevens," he replied in a measured, friendly voice. He opened the vest, reached into his shirt pocket, and took out a thin leather case. He flipped it open with practiced ease. A gold badge glinted in the harsh, fluorescent light. "I'm the town sheriff. I was visiting a friend here when you boys came in with K.D."

"I guess you heard us say that somebody shot her," Frank said. "And I guess you've been sitting there, sizing us up before you identified yourself."

The sheriff offered a lazy smile. "After twenty years on the job, you learn a few tricks that cut through the preliminaries." There was a sparkle in the man's deep-set eyes that told Frank he was still sizing them up.

"I'm Frank Hardy, and this is my brother, Joe," said Frank. "We're here on vacation."

"So you boys found K.D., is that right?" Stevens continued after a brief pause.

"That's right," Joe answered. "You talk like you know her."

The sheriff chuckled softly. "Everybody around

here knows K.D. Her father was one of the biggest ranchers in the state.

"And now that I've answered your question, mind if I ask a few?"

"Fire away," Joe replied.

"What were you doing out in the mountains?"

"Skiing," Frank said simply.

"Where exactly?" the sheriff asked.

Frank got out his map and showed the sheriff where they had found K.D. and where they had been skiing.

The sheriff studied the two brothers silently for a minute. "You weren't doing a little hunting, maybe? You didn't maybe accidentally shoot her?"

Frank wasn't really surprised by the question. He knew that a good detective always looks for the simplest explanation first, and he suspected that Stevens was a fairly effective investigator, in his own way.

"No," he responded calmly. "We're not hunters. You can check our gear if you want. You won't find anything remotely connected to hunting."

Stevens shrugged. "I don't think that'll be necessary. You don't act like a couple of boys staring up out of a deep hole, trying to figure a way to squirm out." He stroked his mustache thoughtfully. "What time did you find her?"

"Assuming my watch is accurate," Frank said, "it was eleven-seventeen."

Joe was surprised. There was so much going on when they found Becker, it would never have occurred to him to check the time. Then he reminded himself that checking the time was the kind of thing that Frank would automatically do, even in a nuclear attack.

"That means you got there about a half hour after the shooting," the sheriff said.

Frank looked at him. "We figured she was shot this morning because she wasn't buried deep in snow, but how did you know the exact time?"

"She was wearing a watch," Stevens explained. "It stopped at ten forty-six. The face was smashed, so I figure it broke when she fell."

This information startled Frank. He had missed the watch completely. He called up a mental image of the crime scene. Becker had been wearing gloves, so the watch would have been covered, and he wouldn't have seen it. Still, something didn't quite fit.

Frank's thoughts were cut off when a tall man wearing a ski jacket burst into the waiting room. He stared briefly at the Hardys and then turned to the sheriff. "I came to find out about K.D.," he said. "How is she?"

Frank studied the newcomer. He had ice blue eyes and short, light brown hair. He had the wiry build of a marathon runner, and his deeply tanned face spoke of long hours in the winter sun and wind.

"She's not in very good shape," the sheriff said candidly. "At least she's alive, thanks to these boys here. Dick Oberman, say hello to Frank and Joe Hardy. Why don't you all get acquainted while I go check on a few details." He paused in the doorway and glanced back over his shoulder. "I'm sure you boys will still be here when I get back, right?" He left without waiting for a response.

Oberman gave the Hardys a puzzled look. "I don't understand. Were you working with K.D.?"

"We just happened to be in the neighborhood at the right time," Joe answered. "Are you her husband?"

That brought a slight smile to the man's strained features. "No. She's married to those mountain lions. But we've been friends a long time. I even spent a few summers helping her with her research."

"Can you think of anyone who might want to hurt her for any reason?" Frank asked.

Oberman's eyes widened. "You think somebody shot her deliberately?"

"I wouldn't rule it out," Frank replied. "What do you think?"

Oberman moved over to the window and gazed out at the mountains. "I guess it's possible," he said in a hesitant tone. "This is mostly a cattle town, and to a rancher a cougar is just a large pest that preys on his livestock. K.D. is trying to protect the cougars. Hunting them is already restricted to one cat per hunter during a limited winter season, but K.D. thinks that's too much. She's been working with an animal rights group in Washington to set up a protected reserve in the national forest. This has some of the local cattle barons pretty hot."

"Anybody in particular?" Frank asked.

"Well," Oberman said slowly, "the biggest rancher in the area is Walt Crawford, and he's had more than one run-in with K.D. She even tried to get him arrested once because she claimed his men were poaching cats out of season. She couldn't prove it, and nobody was ever arrested."

"Anybody else?" Frank pressed.

"Yes," Oberman answered after a slight pause. "There's Ted Gentry, a Native American who's trying to reclaim a big chunk of the national forest for the Ute tribe, including the area that K.D. and her group are fighting for."

Joe frowned. "Gentry doesn't sound like an Indian name."

"It's not," Oberman replied. "His mother was a full-blooded Ute, but his father was white, from one of the old cattle families."

"I should have guessed," Joe muttered. "Is there anybody around here who isn't connected with cows?"

Oberman smiled. "They're cattle—not cows.

But I'm not connected with them in any way. I run a camping supply store here in town."

"We could use some new gear," Frank said. "Maybe we'll come by your store, if we have time before we go home."

"Oh, I don't think you'll be going home just yet," Sheriff Stevens commented from the doorway. The Hardys had no idea how long he had been standing there listening to their conversation.

"We've got some unfinished business," he added with a frown. There was certainly nothing friendly about the two stone-faced deputies standing behind him. Stevens nodded to Frank and Joe. "You boys had better come along with us."

Chapter 4

"IF YOU'RE GOING to arrest us," Frank said in a steady voice, looking straight into the sheriff's eyes, "you'd better have some good evidence."

"Arrest you?" the sheriff responded, raising his bushy eyebrows. "Why would I do that? I just wanted you to know that I booked a room for you at the Tri-Star Motel, compliments of the city." He jerked his thumb over his shoulder at the two deputies. "Harlan here will drive you there, and Gary will bring your car over directly."

Frank knew that "directly" meant after a complete search. He also knew that Stevens would probably back off if the Hardys refused to play along, but he kept his mouth shut and indicated to Joe that he was to do the same. For the time being, it was best to stay on the sheriff's good side. It also wouldn't hurt to let Stevens think he had outwitted the teenage "boys."

Harlan, the taciturn deputy in the creaky leather jacket with a fleece lining, knocked on the Hardys' room door at exactly seven the next morning.

"Some vacation this turned out to be," Joe grumbled as the deputy drove them to an undisclosed destination.

It turned out to be a helipad, located just behind the hospital. There was a helicopter waiting, the rotor already slicing through the crisp morning air. Frank noted that the chopper didn't have any identifying markings. Inside were the pilot and Sheriff Stevens.

The Hardys wedged into the cramped backseat and covered their ears with headsets just like the ones the sheriff and pilot were wearing. The large, cupped headphones and the microphones made it possible to carry on a conversation over the thundering clatter of the whirling rotor blades.

"For a small town, you sure have a fancy hospital," Frank commented.

"The hospital serves the whole county," Stevens explained. "The landing pad is for ambulance choppers. This bird is just a loaner, compliments of a friend."

"So where are we going?" Joe asked.

"Do you really need to ask?" The sheriff's voice sounded loud in his ears.

Joe shrugged to himself. The sheriff was right. He did know the itinerary for this trip.

The route that had taken the Hardys hours took only a few minutes by helicopter. Stevens motioned the pilot to land a healthy distance from the site of the shooting. They walked up to the site, following the ruts carved by the Hardys' skis the previous day.

The sheriff made a quick tour of the area, stooping down every now and then to take closer looks. When he got to the bloodstained spot near the pine tree, he stopped and did a slow, complete turn, scanning the canyon from all sides. "This is where you found her, right?"

"That's right," Joe said.

The sheriff tipped back his hat and scratched his head. "Well, I think we can safely say that nobody strolled up and shot her at point-blank range."

"What makes you so sure of that?" Joe asked.

"Because there are only two sets of tracks," Frank answered. "The ones you and I made yesterday."

"It was probably a stray bullet from some hunter who didn't know he'd hit anything," Stevens said.

"I don't think so," Frank responded.

The sheriff raised his eyebrows. "Why not?"

"You already know why," Frank said bluntly. "Since there aren't any tracks down here, the shooter must have been somewhere up along the canyon wall. He would have had a clear view of the area after the snowstorm." There was something about what he'd just said that didn't ring true to Frank, but he couldn't bring it to the front of his mind.

"It was an accident," Stevens said. "Because right now I don't have a better explanation." He looked at the Hardys. "You boys are free to leave town whenever you want."

"We'll think about it," Joe said.

They spent a few more minutes going over the site. Frank could tell that the sheriff wasn't putting a lot of effort into the search. His mind was already made up.

The morning was still young when the Hardys found themselves back at their motel. Frank had a theory about why the sheriff was reluctant to give the case a lot of attention. "The rancher that Dick Oberman told us about—Walt Crawford—probably has a lot of influence around here," he ventured.

"So even if Stevens did suspect him," Joe said, picking up his brother's idea, "he just might not investigate fully."

"Something like that," Frank agreed. "But I do think he'd go after Crawford with everything he's got if he thought he could make the case stick."

A wide grin spread across Joe's face. "Looks like it's time to trade in our skis for spurs and go round up some 'cows' for questioning."

Crawford's ranch wasn't hard to find. In fact, it probably would have been difficult to find anybody in Elk Springs who *didn't* know how to get to the two-thousand-acre spread called the Lazy W.

It wasn't an exact duplicate of the Old West ranch that Joe had conjured up in his head. The sprawling log house, barn, and bunkhouse inside the main gate fit the image perfectly, but the snowmobiles and all-terrain vehicles brought the picture squarely into the late twentieth century.

The guard at the gate looked like a cowboy with his Stetson and blue jeans. The only difference was that the belt strapped around his waist held a walkie-talkie instead of a six-shooter. Frank drove past the gate without stopping.

"Correct me if I'm wrong," Joe said, "but didn't we just pass the place we're looking for?"

"I'm always happy to correct you when you're wrong," Frank replied amiably. "Sometimes it's a full-time job." He steered the rented sedan around a few turns and glanced in the rearview mirror before pulling over to the side of the road in a wooded area. "Did you think we'd just drive up to the front door and then be invited in?''

Joe zipped up his parka, yanked his ski cap down over his ears, and stuffed his hands in his thick gloves. ''I thought it was worth a shot,'' he grumbled as he opened the door to an icy blast of wind.

They hopped over a low barbed-wire fence, which was built to keep cows in and not people out, and then trudged through the woods toward the house. Joe could feel the cold seeping in through his several layers of clothes as they stalked up to the bunkhouse at the edge of the clearing.

''What are we looking for?'' he asked, stomping his feet while Frank carefully studied the layout of the small complex of buildings.

''I don't know,'' Frank admitted with a casual shrug. ''I thought we should take a look around. If we don't find anything, we'll go see Mr. Crawford and just ask him if he's shot any wildlife researchers lately.''

''Okay,'' Joe muttered, watching the plumes of his breath crystallize into tiny weather systems. ''I get the point.''

Two ranch hands came out of the bunkhouse and walked over to one of the snowmobiles parked nearby. They were both carrying rifles. Frank and Joe quickly ducked behind a thick tree trunk in the shade of the forest.

"I hope we get lucky today," one of the men said. "I sure could use the extra cash."

"I know what you mean," the other one said as he fitted his rifle into a leather case strapped to the vehicle. He swung a leg over the side, settled into the seat, and slid the key into the ignition in a single, easy motion. "If Mr. Crawford paid the bounty by the pound instead of by the head," he shouted as he revved the engine, "the tracks I spotted this morning could lead us to a small fortune. Those paw prints were made by one big old cougar."

Frank and Joe were both remembering what Dick Oberman had told them about the strict controls on hunting mountain lions.

"If Crawford is paying his men a bounty to kill cougars . . ." Frank began.

"And if K. D. Becker caught them in the act—" Joe continued.

The end of the sentence was abruptly cut off by a high-pitched drone from the woods behind them. Frank and Joe spun around as the steady noise grew louder. They had no place to hide.

They didn't even see the snowmobile until it was almost on top of them. "Whoa!" the driver cried out, skidding to a halt as the Hardys dove off to the side. "I almost turned you boys into a hood orna—"

He cut himself off, whipped off his mirrored sunglasses, and squinted at the Hardys suspiciously. "I don't believe I know you young fellas," he said sternly. "What are you doing around here?"

"We're with the federal safety bureau," Joe said, stomping boldy toward the snowmobile. "Why doesn't this vehicle have a seat belt?"

The man's eyes narrowed. "Hey, boys!" he called out sharply. "Get out here and give me a hand! Looks like we caught us a couple of tres-pass—"

The man interrupted himself by jumping off the snowmobile and lunging for Joe. Meaty hands were around Joe's neck in an instant. Joe reacted instinctively and dropped to his knees. The man loosened his grip and Joe squirmed away.

Frank moved without thinking and jumped on the snowmobile, grabbed the controls, and gunned the throttle. "Come on!" he shouted. "Let's get out of here!"

Joe hopped on behind his brother. The snow-mobile lurched forward as the studded treads churned through the snow and spewed out a coarse spray that showered the stunned ranch hand.

The only thing wrong with the escape, Frank realized as they shot out into the open, was that they were headed the wrong way. He spun the snowmobile around, just as a bunch of men poured out of the bunkhouse to find out what the ruckus was all about.

"What's going on here?" Frank heard someone yell. "Stop those boys!"

"Hang on!" Frank shouted, jerking the handlebars and swerving off across an open field, almost losing his brother in the process.

Joe tightened his grip as the snowmobile flew over a small hillock, airborne for a brief moment before it slammed back to earth with a jarring thud. Under better circumstances, he tried to convince himself, this might actually be fun.

His exercise in positive thinking was cut short when the snowmobile twisted violently and jolted to an abrupt stop. Joe lost his grip and pitched off headfirst into the snow.

Frank leapt off the snowmobile and yanked his brother to his feet. "Are you all right?"

Joe gave a shaky nod. "I think so. What happened?"

Frank pointed straight ahead, the way they had been aimed. "That's what happened."

Joe stared into the empty space. His eyes drifted downward, then bulged out in alarm. A few feet from where they had plowed to a stop, the world dropped away over a steep, bleak cliff.

Behind them they could hear the angry whine of snowmobiles and the coarse rumble of all-terrain vehicles. They were closing in for the kill.

Chapter 5

JOE SMILED WEAKLY at his brother. "I don't suppose you brought a very long rope ladder."

Frank moved forward and stared down into the harsh shadows of the deep canyon. "I don't think they make one long enough," he replied grimly.

Joe joined his brother at the edge and peered over. The constant wind howling down the canyon had blown the snow off the cliffside, exposing jagged, barren rocks. He took a deep breath and started moving forward before his brain had a chance to complain.

"Don't even think about doing it," Frank warned as Joe started to lower himself over the edge. "We have to be at least one hundred feet up."

"We have no choice," Joe said, grinning up at his brother as he slowly worked his way down. "This sort of thing is much easier if you don't think about it."

Frank debated—and quickly rejected—grabbing his brother and hauling him back up. One wrong move could get them both killed. "This is a bad idea," he said firmly.

"Probably," Joe admitted, probing the cracks for his next foothold and hoping he wouldn't find ice instead. "But it was the only one I had."

Roaring engines and harsh shouts signaled that Crawford's men would be arriving soon. Frank glanced over his shoulder and decided not to hang around to find out what they'd do if they caught him.

"Race you to the bottom," Joe called up when he saw his brother start to climb down after him.

"No way!" Frank shouted back. "You'd probably jump just to beat me!"

Nobody else took up the challenge, and soon the cowboys' derisive yells dwindled away, drowned out by the whistling winds. Joe moved slowly, selecting his footholds carefully. Although he was anxious to reach the bottom, he knew that one careless move on a patch of ice could lead to disaster. Halfway down, Joe resolved that he'd never take up rock climbing as a hobby. Near the bottom, he decided it wasn't really all that bad. By the time his feet hit the deep snow on the ground, he had convinced himself that it might even be fun.

Any happy thoughts Frank might have had as he reached the bottom were blotted out by a dark shadow and a loud thrumming noise overhead. He glanced up and discovered what the underside of a helicopter looked like. It hovered for a moment before swinging away and landing on a flat stretch of ground a short distance from them.

Joe sighed. "Oh, well, at least we won't have to worry about how we're going to get out of here." He took a harder look at the unmarked helicopter. "Haven't we seen that bird somewhere before?"

Frank nodded. "That's the chopper we took this morning."

The helicopter just squatted there like some fat, ugly bug, the rotor blades spinning round in a hectic blur, whipping up whirlwinds of snow from the ground. The Hardys watched and waited as the door swung open. They waited some more. After a minute or so, they realized that no one was getting out. They were expected to go to the helicopter.

Frank raised his eyebrows, and Joe responded with a shrug. Side by side, they plodded over to the cold steel bird, heads low against the icy sting of the man-made wind.

Frank poked his head inside the cockpit. The pilot gave him a smug grin. "Can I give you boys a lift?" he shouted over the clatter of the turbine engine.

"Do we have any choice?" Frank responded. He was mildly surprised that the pilot was alone in the cockpit.

The pilot's grin widened. "Not really." He patted the empty seat next to him. "Come on. Don't be sore losers."

Frank hadn't paid much attention to the pilot the last time. If he had, he might have noticed the sideways letter *W* that was stitched across the front of his visored cap, confirming what Frank had concluded the moment the chopper swooped down. "So this rig belongs to the Lazy W ranch," he said as he climbed in.

The man sitting at the controls nodded. "Yep. She's only a few weeks old. We haven't gotten around to branding her yet."

Frank crawled into the backseat, and Joe strapped himself in next to the pilot. "Walt Crawford must be a very rich man," he said bluntly as the helicopter took off. "A private helicopter and a pilot to go with it can't be cheap."

"You're right about the bird," the pilot answered. "But I don't charge Mr. Crawford a penny to fly it for him."

Joe gave him a puzzled look. "Why not?"

The pilot responded with a chilly smile. "Because I *am* Walt Crawford."

That put a lid on the conversation for the rest

of the short flight back to the ranch. Frank used the time to make a careful study of the rancher.

Crawford handled the helicopter with relaxed grace, probably reflecting years of practical experience. Frank guessed the clean-shaven, sharp-jawed pilot was around forty-five or fifty years old. A closer look revealed a hint of slack skin and wrinkles where his neck disappeared under his coat collar. Frank upped his age estimate to a healthy sixty.

They touched down on a patch of ground surrounded by a circular driveway that led to an expansive, two-story log house. A boxy, four-door jeep with fat, oversize tires rolled up the drive as the Hardys hopped out of the helicopter. The pair of blue emergency lights perched on the jeep's roof announced that this was not a casual visitor.

Sheriff Stevens burst out of the jeep, and he did not look like a happy man. "I was hoping you boys would be halfway to Denver by now," he said with a stern scowl.

"We get a special rate if we keep the car for a week," Joe quipped. "Our travel agent told us we'd have to pay a substantial penalty if we changed our airline reservations, so we decided to hang around for the rest of the week."

"You may be here a lot longer than that," the sheriff replied. "I hear you stole a snowmobile. That's grand theft. A conviction would get you an extended vacation at one of the state's finest penal resorts."

"Now, hold on Bruce," the rancher spoke up. "When I called you, I thought my men had cornered a couple of cattle rustlers. I didn't realize they were the same brave boys who saved Ms. Becker. I'm sure there's a reasonable explanation for their actions."

The sheriff glowered at the Hardys. "I'm eager to hear it."

Frank turned his steady gaze on Crawford. "I think it would be more interesting to hear your reasonable explanation for paying your men to hunt down mountain lions. I bet that's a felony, too." He glanced over at the sheriff. "Unless some people are above the law."

"Not in my jurisdiction," the sheriff replied flatly.

"I'm afraid there's been a simple misunderstanding," the rancher said smoothly to Bruce Stevens. "I told you about that old tomcat that's been preying on my herd. He got a heifer the day before yesterday, and just the scent of him makes the cattle skittish. Maybe next time he'll cause a stampede or go after one of the men."

The sheriff cut him off with a disgruntled sigh. "So you offered a bonus to any man who could take care of the problem, and the only way to do that is to kill the cat. We've been through this before, Walt. You know I don't like it."

Joe stared at the sheriff in disbelief. "You don't *like* it? That's *all?*"

"There's not much I can do," the sheriff answered. "There's no crime in shooting a cougar on private property if the cat is a threat to people and livestock."

"My men know," Crawford added, "that they're authorized to shoot only if the cat is on my land. Anyplace else is off limits. Those are my strict orders."

"But you have no way of knowing if they'll obey your orders," Frank countered. "They haul in a dead mountain lion, tell you they bagged it on the ranch, and you just take their word for it and pay them."

The rancher smiled thinly. "I trust my men, and I trust that you won't cause any more unwarranted trouble. I'm going to forget this whole trespassing and theft incident."

"That's fine with me," the sheriff responded. "It's a lot less paperwork if I don't have to arrest these boys. Come on, I'll give you two a lift back to your car," Stevens said.

Frank and Joe said their goodbyes and piled into the sheriff's car.

"Did you believe his story?" Joe demanded.

"More or less," the sheriff replied.

"What does that mean?"

"It means I think Crawford's men probably bend the rules a little sometimes, and he looks the other way."

"And what do you think would happen if somebody like K. D. Becker caught them in the act?" Frank prodded.

"I don't know," Stevens said. "And since she was shot roughly thirty-five miles away from the Lazy W Ranch, I'm not going to give it much thought."

"Maybe Crawford was offering a bonus on more than cougars," Joe suggested.

The sheriff shook his head slowly. "K. D. Becker is a nuisance to Walt Crawford, and that's about all. Her big campaign to save the cougars won't put much of a dent in his cattle ranching business.

"Besides," he continued patiently, "this isn't exactly the criminal underworld we're dealing with here. Walt Crawford is a respected rancher, and his men are basically honest, hardworking cowboys."

Frank wondered whether the sheriff was blind to Crawford, since the two were friends.

"And before you ask," Stevens added, "Walt Crawford was in Montana yesterday at a cattle auction. So unless he's a really good shot, I think we can safely assume that he didn't pull the trigger."

"Speaking of shots," Frank responded, "do you have any idea what kind of gun was used in the shooting?"

The sheriff nodded. "We're not sure of the exact caliber yet. Preliminary ballistics tests on the slug the doctor took out of K.D. indicate a high-power hunting rifle. Since the bullet didn't penetrate very deep—"

"It was probably shot from a long distance," Frank cut in, finishing the sentence. "Any closer, and she wouldn't be alive."

The sheriff stopped the jeep next to the Hardys' car. He turned his head and gave Frank a curious look. "You're just full of surprises, aren't you? Where'd you learn that stuff?"

"He just has a bright, inquisitive mind," Joe said offhandedly.

"I don't doubt it," the sheriff replied, his eyes still on Frank. "And does that bright mind find anything inconsistent with the theory of a simple hunting accident?"

"No," Frank readily admitted. "Are you checking out hunting parties that might have been in the area?"

"That's what they pay me for," the sheriff said with more than a hint of impatience. "I'm also working on some other leads."

"Like what?" Joe asked.

The two-way radio clamped to the dashboard squawked just then. "Ah, come in, Sheriff Stevens—do you copy? This is Alpha Tango One Niner—"

The sheriff grabbed the handset and thumbed the Talk button. "I don't need your license plate number, Harlan. What have you got for me? Did you find anything?"

"Ah, that's a roger," the radio crackled.

"Speak English," the sheriff snapped. "Did you find the rifle or not?"

"Yes, sir," the static-filled voice replied. "It was right where you told me to look."

"Okay," Stevens said. "Take it down to headquarters. I'll be there in a little while." He hung up the handset without waiting for a response.

"What was that all about?" Joe asked.

"Looks like your theory about somebody deliberately trying to kill K.D. may be right," the sheriff answered. "If this lead checks out, I'll have the culprit behind bars within twenty-four hours."

Chapter 6

"HOW DID YOU FIND the weapon?" Frank asked. "Did it just turn itself in?"

"Did you know," the sheriff replied in his relaxed drawl, "that most criminals are caught because someone they know turns them in?"

"So who shot Becker?" Joe responded. "And who turned him in?"

"The *alleged* perpetrator," the sheriff said carefully, "is a Native American activist named Ted Gentry. The name probably doesn't mean anything to you. I doubt if he's made headlines outside our immediate area."

"We know who he is," Frank said. "What makes you think he's your man?"

"I got an anonymous phone tip," Stevens explained. "The caller said he heard a shot and saw Gentry leave the canyon where K.D. was found. Then he said he found a rifle stashed in Gentry's truck. Harlan picked up the rifle and says it was fired recently."

Frank frowned. "That doesn't make a lot of sense. Why would Gentry drive around with the rifle? You'd think he'd hide it."

"Maybe he did, sort of," the sheriff replied. "His cabin is off the beaten path, and no one plows his road, so Gentry stores his truck in a garage in town during the winter and gets around on skis and with help from his friends. He probably thought the rifle would be safe there."

"And maybe somebody set him up," Joe countered. "Doesn't just about everyone have a hunting rifle in Elk Springs? How do you know his is the right rifle? Maybe it's not even his rifle."

The sheriff grunted. "You boys don't give up, do you? What do you want me to do—arrest every single person in Elk Springs?"

"We just want to make sure you get the right man," Frank answered.

"Or woman," Joe added.

"I'll tell you what," the sheriff said coolly. "I'll track down the criminals, and you boys go do whatever it is teenagers do."

"So you haven't arrested Gentry yet?" Frank prodded.

"No," Stevens said. "But I plan to have a talk with him as soon as I ditch the two of you." He nodded out the window. "There's your car.

Get in it and go someplace—anyplace. I don't care where, just as long as you're out of my hair."

The Hardys took the hint.

"So what do we do now?" Joe asked as they sat in their car and watched the sheriff's jeep roll off down the road.

Frank started the engine. "We do exactly what the sheriff said." There was a glint in his eyes.

Joe smiled. "Right. We stay out of his hair, but we don't let him get out of sight."

Frank was careful to keep distance between them and the jeep. As there was very little traffic, nothing but empty road separated the two vehicles.

"Boy, he sure wasn't kidding about Gentry living off the beaten path," Joe observed as they bumped along a twisting mountain road.

"He's got to know we're following him," Frank said pensively. "If he hasn't noticed us by now, his rearview mirror must have fallen off."

"Do you think he's leading us on a wild-goose chase?" Joe ventured.

Frank shook his head. "I doubt it. I don't think he'd waste that kind of time."

The jeep disappeared around a sharp curve, but Frank wasn't worried. It would come back into view when the sedan poked around the bend. At least, that's what he assumed. But on the other side of the curve there was nothing but empty road. The jeep was gone.

Joe, eyes wide, jerked his head from side to side. "What happened? Where'd he go?"

Frank stopped the car, his eyes making a detailed sweep of both sides of the road. He twisted around and stared back toward the curve.

"I should have known," he muttered when he saw the new set of tire tracks in the snow snaking up a steep incline through a long, narrow clearing in the trees. "Sheriff Stevens told us Gentry lived off the beaten path—on an unplowed road."

"No wonder the sheriff wasn't worried about us following him," Joe said. "With four-wheel drive and huge snow tires, Stevens doesn't even need a road, plowed or not. But we wouldn't get ten feet up that path in this thing."

"Then we'll just have to leave the car here," Frank said simply.

Joe gaped at his brother. "You mean we're going to walk? We don't know how far it is to Gentry's cabin."

"We'll know when we get there," Frank replied. He got out of the car and patted the ski rack on the roof. "If you don't like walking, there are other ways to get around in the snow."

Joe wasn't sure which would be worse, slogging through knee-deep snow or sidestepping with long cross-country skis uphill. He took another look at the narrow path and convinced himself that the slope flattened out beyond the first bend. "Oh, well," he said as he helped his brother get out their gear. "We came here to ski, so let's do it."

They didn't get far before the jeep with police lights and big, fat, knobby tires came rumbling back down the trail and stopped a few inches from the tips of Joe's skis. The sheriff stuck his head out the window. His face held a mix of emotions, as if he couldn't decide whether to laugh at the persistent pair or lock them up.

"Beautiful scenery around here," Joe remarked nonchalantly. "Did you come up to see some natural wonder, like we did?"

The sheriff struggled to suppress a grin. "You boys sure have a lot of spunk," he said. "I'll give you that." He took off his cowboy hat and wiped his forehead with the back of his hand. "I hate to tell you that you're wasting your time, though. Mr. Gentry isn't at home today."

Joe pursed his lips in a pout. "Aw, shucks. No one there to buy our Boy Scout cookies?"

"Fun's fun," the sheriff responded, shifting into a serious tone, "but this is police business. Gentry may be armed and dangerous."

"All you have so far is a rifle that *might* belong to Gentry and *might* be the one used in the shooting," Frank pointed out. "That's not exactly what I'd call any kind of case against him.''

''I've found it's always safest to assume the worst,'' the sheriff replied. He paused and scratched his thick mustache. ''You'll live longer that way.''

''You're probably right,'' Frank said in a subdued voice. He didn't want to start an argument after they'd managed to get the sheriff in a relatively good mood.

The sheriff eyed him warily. ''I should escort you boys off this mountain.'' He glanced down at his watch. ''But I don't have time. So you're on your own. Try to stay out of trouble.

''And stay clear of Gentry's place!'' he shouted back out the window as he drove off.

Frank and Joe smiled cheerfully and waved goodbye vigorously. As soon as the jeep was out of sight, they continued up the trail.

As Joe had hoped, the steep grade soon tapered off. It was still mostly uphill, but by cutting diagonally back and forth across the rise, they made pretty good time. ''This is like trying to run a marathon on your hands,'' Joe panted after about a half hour.

''I know,'' Frank huffed. ''There's nothing quite like it to keep the old cardiovascular system in shape.''

''Yeah, right,'' Joe grumbled. ''There's nothing like giving yourself a heart attack now to prevent having one later.''

Frank stopped and turned to smile at Joe. "If you can't handle it, I can go on by myself. Just go back to the car and wait for me. It's all downhill from here."

Joe couldn't ignore the challenge. "I'm fine," he said with a forced grin. "I was just worried about you."

Soon they were both furiously stabbing the snow with their poles and racing straight up the trail in a silent duel. That was how they worked. They pushed each other to stretch their limits and then go a little further. Other people saw only a couple of teenagers. They didn't see the serious, dedicated detective team.

The trail left the woods, and the furrows in the snow meandered across a wide, flat meadow. Frank didn't need a compass to know what direction they were going. They were chasing the late-afternoon sun, already low in the western sky.

Too low, Frank told himself. He stopped and checked his watch. "Time for a break!" he called out as Joe shot ahead.

Joe glided to a halt and looked back over his shoulder. "What's the matter? Can't keep up with me?"

Frank shook his head. "I can't keep up with the sun, and neither can you. We've got to go back."

Joe shielded his eyes with a cupped hand and squinted ahead. "We can't stop now," he protested. "We've got to be close. It didn't take Sheriff Stevens that long to drive there and back. Gentry's cabin is probably right over that next rise."

"It'll still be there tomorrow," Frank replied. "After dark we could freeze to death out here without any protection."

Joe had to admit that his brother was right. Reluctantly, he swung around and followed Frank out of the meadow and back into the trees.

The shaded pine forest was dark compared to the glare off the stark white meadow. Joe shivered with a sudden chill. He tried to shake it off, but the effort made him dizzy. He staggered and groped for a nearby tree trunk. He leaned against it heavily and gulped air.

Frank came over and gently took hold of his arm to steady him. "Relax and take slow, deep breaths. You probably have a mild case of overexertion. Remember this is thin mountain air. It can sneak up on you sometimes."

Joe nodded slowly. The woozy, spinning feeling gradually faded. He was feeling almost normal when he heard a rustling in the branches above him.

Frank heard it, too. He raised his head and caught a glimpse of movement.

"What is it?" Joe whispered hoarsely.

Frank put a finger to his lips and kept his eyes on the tree limbs overhead.

"I have a bad feeling about this," Joe muttered softly.

Frank stared intently, trying to see through the tangled network of branches and pine boughs. There was another faint rustling—then a branch creaked. Something was definitely moving around up there—something large. Suddenly a dark shape appeared over Frank's head in a blur of motion and hurtled straight down toward him.

Chapter 7

FRANK DOVE out of the path of the plummeting shape. As a muffled thud sounded behind him, Frank unfastened his skis and steeled himself, grimly prepared for the worst.

He wasn't prepared for what did happen next, though.

"Um—hi there," Joe ventured in a tentative voice. "I'm Joe Hardy. That guy sprawled in the snow over there is my brother, Frank."

Frank twisted around and saw the back of a figure clad in winter camouflage towering over his brother. A long, jet black ponytail hung down his back and stood out against the mottled streaks of brown, green, and white. An elaborately curved hunting bow with a steel cable drawstring was slung over one shoulder.

A serious face with keen, black eyes turned to scrutinize Frank. "This is private property," the man announced in a deep, resonant voice.

"Sorry," Frank said as he got up. "We didn't see any signs."

"I don't believe in them," the man said. "Barbed wire fences and ugly, hostile signs mar the beauty of the land. People should respect the rights of others without threats.

"No trespassing. Violators will be prosecuted," he intoned derisively. "Where was our fine legal system when the white man was violating Native American land?"

"You must be Ted Gentry," Frank responded, avoiding the question since he didn't have a good answer.

The man nodded. "Now that we've all been properly introduced, perhaps you could tell me what you're doing here."

"Looking for you," Joe replied.

"I seem to be a popular guy today," Gentry remarked. "First Sheriff Stevens, and now you."

"You saw the sheriff?" Joe asked.

Gentry gestured at the tread marks in the snow. "I didn't actually see him, but I do recognize the tracks." His dark eyes flicked between the two brothers. "I don't suppose you'd have any idea why the sheriff drove all the way up here to see me?"

Frank decided to gamble with the truth. "He

wanted to question you about the shooting of K. D. Becker."

Gentry focused his full attention on Frank. "I just heard about K.D. today—a friend let me know on the shortwave. But what makes Stevens think I know anything about it?"

"They found a rifle in your truck," Frank explained. "They think it might be the weapon used in the attack."

Gentry let out a short, bitter laugh. "Without my truck I'm restricted to skis, which I'm not great on. How could I have skied out to shoot K.D.—in a snowstorm—and then skied back to town to hide a rifle in my own truck? Why would I hide it there, anyway? Then I supposedly would have to ski all the way back here. You know how far out I live—I'd still be skiing. But who knows, maybe they'll uncover a signed confession before they get around to questioning me.

"By the way, what's your connection to all this?" Gentry asked.

Frank shrugged his shoulders and started to speak.

"Never mind," Gentry said. "I just figured out who you are. You must be the guys who found K.D. and got her to the hospital." Frank and Joe nodded. "Nice work. I hope she pulls through. She's doing such important research, and she's working for a good cause."

"You mean the wildlife refuge?" Frank responded. ‘‘We heard you had other plans for the same land.’’

‘‘Our goals aren’t that far apart,’’ Gentry said. ‘‘The Utes and other tribes lived in harmony with nature for centuries—and we have a special respect for the cougars. We call them the spirit of the mountains.’’

‘‘So you don’t see her as a threat to your claims that the land should be returned to the Utes?’’ Frank probed.

Gentry sighed. ‘‘Just between you and me and the woodchucks, I stand a better chance of winning the state lottery than convincing the federal government to give back *anything* it stole from my people. And if we can’t have our ancestral lands, I wouldn’t mind seeing a piece of it saved for those magnificent beasts.’’

‘‘Okay,’’ Joe said. ‘‘So let’s say you really didn’t have motive or opportunity. What about the rifle in your truck? If ballistics tests indicate it fired the bullet, the sheriff’s still going to ask you to do a lot of explaining. He’ll figure someone could have driven you around.’’

Gentry looked at the sky. ‘‘It’s getting dark,’’ he said. ‘‘I’m ready for a warm fire and a hot dinner. You’re welcome to join me, unless you have other plans.’’

‘‘None that we can think of,’’ Joe said with a smile.

* * *

Gentry's home, nestled in a grove of aspen trees, was a simple, one-story log house. Inside there was a single spacious room with a sleeping loft at one end and a massive stone fireplace at the other. Most of the furniture appeared to be hand carved.

Only three things spoiled the image of its being a rustic cabin: a fairly new refrigerator in one corner, a shortwave radio, and a personal computer perched on the end of a long worktable. "I didn't see any power lines," Joe noted. "Where does the electricity come from?"

"There's a generator powered by an ugly tank of liquid propane out back," Gentry explained, grabbing up an armload of logs from a stack outside. "It also supplies most of the heat. This beautiful old fireplace makes a lousy furnace. Most of the heat goes right up the chimney."

He took a match from the scarred oak mantel and lit the kindling in the grate. "Still, there's nothing like a blazing fire to keep you company when winds howl outside."

Joe warmed his hands by the growing flame. "I know what you mean."

Frank wandered over to the worktable. What had looked like a jumble of rocks and pebbles from the far side of the room resolved themselves into an assortment of small clay pottery shards and stone arrowheads. "Looks like somebody's doing some archaeological research."

"You might call it a hobby of mine," Gentry replied casually.

Frank's eyes moved to the computer. "Just a hobby?"

Gentry smiled. "Okay, you caught me. I'm an escaped college professor. The university became a little too stuffy for me, so I took a sabbatical to become politically active for my tribe."

Frank studied the tall man with the long black hair. 'I'd like to hear more about your politics."

Gentry shrugged his wide, muscular shoulders. "There's not much more to hear. I've been working with a group of tribal activists and lawyers for a few years now. We don't really expect to get our land back. We *do* have a real shot at a financial settlement, though. That would mean better schools, better hospitals, and maybe a chance at a better life for a lot of Native Americans."

"So the land is the focal point of your cause," Frank pointed out. "If Becker gets her wildlife refuge, you'd have a harder time getting public support to return the land to your people."

"I told you before that I'm sympathetic to Becker's cause. I'm also peace loving. Do you honestly think I'd attempt to kill one human being to help others?"

"But what about all these weapons?" Joe asked. He pointed out a rack that held three intricate hunting bows, similar to the one Gentry had been carrying when they met him. They were all compound bows—molded, curved fiberglass jobs with steel cable drawstrings looped around a pulley-like cam assembly at each end. Joe knew the design made them more powerful. It also made them much more deadly.

His eyes moved on. One end of the worktable contained an array of hand tools and a variety of half-finished, high-tech arrows. The coat rack on the wall was made of elk antlers. The rug on the floor might have come from the same animal.

"These are the signs of a serious hunter who knows his business," Joe finished.

"What else?" Gentry prodded.

"Isn't that enough?" Joe replied.

"I think it's what we *don't* see," Frank ventured.

Gentry smiled. "Very good."

"I don't get it," Joe said with a frown.

Frank picked up an arrow with a razor-sharp steel head. "You see all the signs of a dedicated bow hunter. There aren't any guns of any kind. Becker was shot with a rifle."

"Exactly," Gentry said. "I'm a sustenance hunter. I don't hunt for sport. I kill what I need to eat, and I do it the way my ancestors did. I don't own any firearms."

"I doubt if your ancestors had bows like these," Joe said. "Just because we don't see any guns here doesn't mean you don't own one."

"No, it doesn't," Gentry admitted. "But it gives you something to think about." He walked over to the small kitchen area and opened a cupboard above the stove. "I hope you guys like canned beans. Tonight's menu would have included venison. Unfortunately, the main course got wind of me before I could get off a clean shot."

"Whatever you have is fine," Frank said politely.

Joe stretched his arms and yawned. "I think I'm more tired than hungry, anyway. I could probably fall asleep right here in this chair by the fire."

"That's good," Gentry said. "Because those are the best accommodations I have to offer, and you're sort of stuck here until morning."

Joe didn't reply. He was already asleep.

Shortly after sunrise, Frank woke to a gust of arctic air and the sound of the cabin door closing. A note on the table said Gentry had gone out hunting and wouldn't be back until late in the day. It also said they shouldn't have any trouble finding their way back down the trail. The unspoken message was clear: Don't be here when I get back.

That wasn't a problem. Frank was anxious to get back to town. He wanted to find out if there was any improvement in Becker's condition. But to avoid a continuous series of complaints all the way back to the car, he let Joe sleep a while longer.

He decided to enjoy the early-morning daylight and go outside. He was also making a conscious effort not to snoop around the cabin.

Frank quietly opened the door and stepped out onto the porch. He shivered as the frigid mountain air gusted around him. As he started to pull the door shut behind him, a chunk of the door frame next to his head exploded into splinters. A sharp pain sliced through Frank's skull, and the world went black.

Chapter 8

A PEAL OF THUNDER ripped through Joe's dream of a summer day at the beach, jolting him awake.

Someone yelled, "I got him!"

Another voice shouted, "What in tarnation do you think you're doing?"

Joe's bleary eyes slowly focused on a form lying in the cabin doorway. Any hope of returning to sleep was blasted away when the shape resolved itself into a body.

"Frank!" he cried out, leaping to his feet. He rushed to his brother's side, not even considering what might be on the other side of the door.

Joe knelt down and saw a red welt on the side of Frank's head, just above the temple. He heard talking and spotted three armed men coming out of the woods,

Sheriff Stevens threw his hat at one of his deputies. "Put that thing down, Harlan!" he barked. "It might go off again."

The deputy gave him a wounded look. "You said we should consider him armed and dangerous."

The sheriff picked up his cowboy hat and brushed off the snow. "Does either of those boys look like Gentry? Are they armed—with anything?"

Frank groaned and opened his eyes. "What happened?"

"A piece of door frame hit you on the head," Joe answered.

"Shot out by an overanxious deputy," the sheriff said. He was clearly relieved to hear Frank speak.

With Joe's help, Frank struggled to a sitting position. "Yesterday you just wanted to talk to Gentry. Today you shoot first and ask questions later. What's going on? Did ballistics match the rifle with the bullet?" Frank asked.

"The results were inconclusive," the sheriff answered.

"Did you check to make sure Gentry is the registered owner of the rifle?" Joe asked.

"As far as the state computer files are concerned, Ted Gentry doesn't own a gun," Stevens said. "And since the serial number's been filed off the rifle, we may never find out whose name is on the registration. It's a mighty fine weapon, a brand-new bolt-action Winchester with one of those fancy German scopes."

"Let me get this straight," Joe said. "You don't even know if the rifle you have was used in the shooting, or if it belongs to Gentry. So why the trigger-happy posse?"

"We have a witness," the sheriff said.

"Somebody, other than an anonymous caller, who actually saw Gentry shoot Becker?" Frank asked.

"Not exactly," the sheriff replied. "But somebody did see him in the area that morning. A hunting party was camped about three miles north of there. The guide's a local fellow named Mark Pearson. I had paid him a visit to ask if he'd seen anything that might help us out.

"He couldn't recall anything unusual," the sheriff continued. "But he did suggest that I ask Gentry, since he had seen him near the canyon."

"Maybe Pearson is lying because he did the shooting," Joe suggested.

"I thought of that," Stevens replied. "So I checked his story with the folks in the hunting party. They all said the same thing—nobody left the group that morning, and nobody fired a shot."

"But there was a storm that morning—how could any of them have seen anyone until it ended at ten?" Joe asked.

"There was that short period of time when it stopped snowing, around nine," Frank reminded him. Frank then turned to the sheriff with a sharp look. "What were they hunting? Can you tell us that, at least?"

Sheriff Stevens cleared his throat and stood up. "Cougars," he said stiffly. He walked brusquely into the cabin and looked around. "What are you doing here, anyway?"

"Just paying a social visit," Joe said lightly.

The sheriff turned and gave him a cold stare. "I could charge you boys as accessories."

Frank got to his feet slowly, rubbing at the dull ache in his temple. "We could probably sue you for wrongful injury."

The sheriff was silent for a moment. Then he pushed up the brim of his hat and turned on the smile again. "What are we arguing about? We're all on the same side, right? And just to show you there's no hard feelings, let me give you a lift back to your car." His tone said it wasn't a request.

After the sheriff dropped them off, the Hardys drove straight to the Elk Springs Hospital to check on Becker. Dick Oberman was just coming out as they were going in.

"How is she?" Frank asked.

"Stable," Oberman answered. "She's still in a coma."

Frank tried to be optimistic. "At least she's not any worse. If she's stable, she still has a good chance."

"I've heard that talking and reading to coma

victims sometimes helps them recover faster," Joe said. "Maybe we should do that."

Oberman didn't seem very receptive to the idea. "I doubt if they'll even let you see her. An aunt and uncle were here earlier. You're not relatives. You barely even know her. I got in only because I know one of the nurses in the intensive care unit."

"So you can put in a good word for us," Joe said.

Oberman glanced at his watch. "I can't, right now. I've got to get back to the store."

"I almost forgot about that," Frank said. "You have a camping supply store. Is it far from here?"

Oberman laughed. "Nothing's very far from anything else in Elk Springs. It's only a couple blocks away."

"Terrific," Frank said. "I think I could use a new sleeping bag—a much warmer one. Mind if we tag along?"

"Not at all," Oberman replied. "I'll even give you a special discount. I wouldn't want you to leave town without at least one pleasant memory."

"This is my kind of town," Frank remarked as they walked down the street. "Most of these stores look like they've always been here and always will be. There are no instant neon fast-food minimalls. No highrise office complexes."

"No tourist traps hawking genuine Native

American artifacts fresh from Taiwan," Joe added.

Oberman stopped at a storefront with a rustic wooden sign above the door. Carved into the wood was the name Adventure Outfitters. "Well, I wouldn't mind if Elk Springs attracted a *few* more tourists," he said, pushing the door open. "Things may change a lot around here if the new state highway project gets approved."

"If it were easier to get here," Joe argued, "this would turn into another resort town like Aspen."

Oberman smiled. "I think I could live with that."

Frank browsed through the aisles of daypacks and duffel bags, canteens and cook stoves. The rain gear and clothes leaned heavily toward camouflage styles. So did the tents and packs. A locked glass case displayed an assortment of colorful shotgun shells, fat deer slugs, and sleek, steel-jacketed, high-caliber rifle ammunition.

"Are a lot of your customers hunters?" he asked.

Oberman nodded. "Most of my business comes from the hunting crowd. I can't say I understand the appeal. I never got into it, myself."

Joe pointed to a row of trophies on a shelf behind the counter. The largest one was topped with the figure of a man on skis, a rifle slung over his shoulder. "If you're not into hunting, what are those for?"

"Biathlon competition," Oberman explained. "It's a combination of cross-country skiing and target shooting. Most hunters would laugh at the kind of rifle I use—a twenty-two. It's great for target accuracy, but it wouldn't stop anything bigger than a squirrel."

"Isn't the biathlon an Olympic event?" Joe asked.

"That's right," Oberman answered. His voice took on a wistful tone. "In fact, I was on the Olympic team. Well, I was an alternate, anyway. Nobody got sick or broke a leg or anything, so I never got my chance to go for the gold."

"Do you know many of the local hunting guides?" Frank asked, steering the conversation back on track.

"Sure," Oberman said, his eyes still on the trophy case.

"What about Mark Pearson?" Frank asked.

That seemed to get Oberman's attention. "Where did you hear that name?"

"The sheriff told us about him," Joe said. "Pearson claims he saw Ted Gentry near the canyon where K.D. was shot."

"Mark Pearson isn't going to win any awards for honesty," Oberman said. "He used to be a state game warden. He got fired for taking payoffs from hunters who wanted their own private, extended hunting season. Now he runs his own 'big game' operation."

"Do you think he might be lying about Gentry?" Joe responded.

Oberman shrugged his shoulders. "I wouldn't put it past him—if he had a reason." His eyes widened. "You don't think Pearson shot her, do you?"

"It wouldn't hurt to ask," Frank said.

Joe glanced at his brother. "It might—but when has that ever stopped us?"

Oberman gave them directions to Pearson's place, a short distance outside town. As the Hardys neared the old farmhouse, a weathered blue pickup truck with a trailer attached drove out of the driveway. There were three men in the cab. The bed of the truck was loaded with crates of some kind, and the trailer carried two black snowmobiles.

Frank slowed and let the truck gain some distance. "Looks like the intrepid guide is on the job," he said. "If we stick with him, maybe we can pick up a few tips on hunting safety."

Joe grinned. "There's no telling what you might learn if you keep your eyes open and pay attention."

Frank matched the truck's speed but hung back, following from a safe distance.

"If you let them get any farther ahead," Joe remarked, "they'll be in a different time zone."

"I don't want them to spot us," Frank replied.

"If we're very careful and a little lucky, they may not notice anything behind them."

The truck slowly weaved along the snowy and icy mountain roads and eventually pulled off to the side on a high ridge. Frank quickly backed his car around a curve and out of sight. He grabbed his pack out of the backseat and fished out the monocular.

Hiding in a jumble of boulders, the two brothers took turns with the palm-size telescope, watching the action around the truck. After unloading the snowmobiles from the trailer, a heavyset man with a rusty red beard jumped into the bed of the truck.

"That must be Pearson," Frank whispered as he peered through the magnifying lens. He took a close look at one of the crates and realized what it was, just as the burly man flung it open and the contents bounded out. "Dog carriers," he murmured, handing the monocular to Joe.

By the time Joe brought the scene into focus, a half dozen brown-and-white-spotted beagles with floppy ears and frantic tails were leaping out of the truck and scampering in the snow. The bearded man jumped down to the ground and walked around to the cab. He took out something that almost made Joe drop the compact telescope.

Joe gave his brother a sharp nudge and thrust the monocular back in his face. "Take a look at this," he whispered.

Frank peered through the lens, but all he could see was the man's back. Then Pearson started to turn slowly, as if he were looking for something small and hard to find. He continued to circle—and eventually Frank could see what had jolted his brother.

In one hand the man gripped a blue metal box with wires attached to it. With the other hand he was aiming something down the sloping ridge. It was a small arrow-shaped antenna—just like the one K. D. Becker used to track her mountain lions.

Chapter 9

FRANK MET his brother's eyes. "Are you thinking the same thing I'm thinking?"

"He's not using that thing to tune in the Weather Channel," Joe replied. "I also don't think this kind of hunting is much of a sport."

Frank nodded. "Exactly what I was thinking."

He took another look through the monocular. The wide man with the thick red beard barked out a few words, and the hounds took off down the slope. Then he loaded a rifle case and some supplies onto the back of one of the snowmobiles. The other two men busied themselves by strapping their own gun cases onto the other snowmobile. The three men had a short conversation. The bearded man waved the antenna around and stared intently at the blue metal box.

He exchanged a few more words with the other men and pointed off in the distance. Then the three of them hopped on and roared away on the two snowmobiles.

Joe jumped up when he heard the engines. "They're getting away!" he shouted.

Frank grabbed his arm and jerked him back down behind the rock. "They'll come back," he said firmly. "If we move fast, we can get the sheriff and bring him back here before they return."

"If we move fast," Joe shot back hotly, "we can stop Pearson before he kills another one of Becker's mountain lions. He might as well shoot animals in the zoo! With their radio collars on, those cats can't hide from him!" He whirled around and stomped off toward the car.

Frank ran after his brother. "What are you going to do?" He had seen that expression on Joe's face before, usually right before Joe did something they were both sorry about later.

"I'm going to do something," Joe growled. He yanked his skis off the rack on top of the car, flung open the trunk, and snatched his ski boots.

"Joe," Frank began, trying to reason with his brother, "they're on snowmobiles, and they have guns—*big* guns with bullets the size of small cruise missiles. We'll never catch them. And if we do, we might end up as tragic victims of a fatal hunting 'accident.' "

Joe ripped off his hiking boots and jammed his feet into his ski boots with fierce, single-minded determination. "I don't care much about hunting one way or the other," he said. The edge in his voice was razor sharp and hard enough to cut glass. "But I like to think that most of the time the animals have a fighting chance."

He stuffed his hands deep into his gloves and curled his fists tightly around his ski poles. "I'm going to do whatever I can to give at least one cougar that fighting chance."

Frank sighed. "Once you get an idea stuck in your head, not even heavy explosives can jar it loose. Hold on while I get my gear. If you're going to get killed, I don't want to be left alive to explain it to Mom and Dad."

They got off to a fast start, going downhill on a steep ridge. They easily followed the snowmobile tracks that snaked along in tandem.

Joe could hear the faint whine of the snowmobiles, the distant sound doubling his determination. "I think we're gaining on them," he said.

Frank didn't answer right away. He didn't want to break his rhythm. He kept his breathing deep and even, planting his poles and moving his skis in a steady flow. "Sound echoes in the hills," he replied, pacing his words between breaths. "They could be miles away."

Joe had already set a fierce pace and was now

pushing himself even harder. "And they might be right around the next bend," he insisted.

Frank didn't bother to respond at all—there was no point. Joe would press ahead until he collapsed. So Frank conserved his energy the best he could and blotted out everything but the smooth pumping of his arms, legs, and lungs. Plant, kick, glide, inhale. Plant, kick, glide, exhale. He bent his head and focused on the back of Joe's skis. Plant, kick, glide, inhale. Plant, kick, glide—

The distant buzz dwindled and died. Joe strained to pick up any sound other than the soft scrape of skis across snow and his own labored breathing. He forced himself to go faster.

The long, snaking ravine that they were skiing now spilled out onto a wide, flat plain. The snowmobile tracks cut a pair of ruler-straight furrows across it. The ground was almost *too* flat, Frank thought. They were in a roughly circular clearing, about a half mile wide. Tall fir, pine, and aspen trees crowded the edges of the clearing, but none strayed out into it.

They weren't in a clearing, Frank realized. They were gliding across the frozen surface of a small mountain lake. If the ice could hold the snowmobiles, it wouldn't even notice the weight of two skiers. And the smooth, flat surface was ideal for cross-country skiing. The only thing easier would be going downhill.

What bothered Frank was the fact that the

lake was sitting at the bottom of a deep basin. Beyond the shoreline, the trees marched sharply up steep slopes. The ravine they had just followed was actually a frozen stream that fed the lake. The lake had been carved out because there was no place else for the water to go. This was the end of the line.

The snowmobile tracks pointed to a narrow break in the trees, and Joe kept his eyes focused on that. For now, that was his goal. He couldn't tell where the trail went from there, although he knew that "up" was likely to be the direction.

When they reached the chilly, dark cover of the trees, the trail was still easy to follow. The tracks veered to the right and then zigzagged up a switchback trail cut into the side of the thickly wooded slope. Joe's eyes traced the path to the rim of the basin, at least a hundred vertical feet above. His heart sank. His arms ached, and his legs felt like rubber. He didn't think he could make the climb without a few minutes' rest to get his wind back. Even then it would be slow going. The hunters would get farther away and closer to their prey.

Just then he heard something, though. A faint but frenzied yapping reverberated in the natural amplifier of the lake basin.

Joe saw his brother's eyes light up, too. "The dogs!" he managed to croak out. He put on a burst of speed, tapping an energy reserve he didn't know he had. Pearson's hounds were somewhere just up ahead, barking wildly.

The scramble up the steep slope took about everything Joe and Frank had left. The effort wasn't wasted, though. From the rim, they had a commanding view down into a shallow valley on the other side of the lake basin. Less than a hundred yards away, a thick slab of rock with sheer sides thrust up ten feet out of the ground. The dogs were doing a skittish dance around the base, hopping and yelping and whacking each other with their whipsaw tails. The three hunters were clustered by the snowmobiles, parked a short distance away from them.

A snarling, hissing mountain lion prowled back and forth across the top of the rock slab. Joe could almost feel the cat's anger and fear. The cougar could easily take out one or two of the hounds, but he couldn't take on the whole pack. They were all around him. There was no place to go. He was trapped.

The hunters didn't even notice the Hardys. They were too busy arguing about something. Joe couldn't make any sense of it. He could hear the angry words, but he was just having a hard time accepting the signals his ears were sending to his brain.

"I saw him first!" one of them snapped. "So he's mine!"

"I don't see your name on him!" the other one barked. He was clutching a rifle in one hand.

"I say he belongs to whoever can shoot him first. So get out of my way!"

The two men started to shove each other, and Joe was sure a slugfest was about to break out. But Pearson stepped neatly between them. "Why don't you flip a coin?" he suggested in a polite but forceful voice.

"Because they've already flipped their minds," Joe muttered.

Frank shot a sidelong glance at his brother. After seventeen years of hanging around with him, he could almost read Joe's mind.

Frank's arm shot out a split second too late. Joe was already moving. His skis skimmed across the snow, picking up speed as he slipped down into the valley. He was going to stop the hunters. He didn't know how. He was just going to do it.

The bearded man had whirled around. There was a huge revolver in his hand. From Joe's angle, the thing looked more like a small cannon. Maybe that was because the barrel was pointed right at Joe's head.

Chapter 10

JOE GRITTED HIS TEETH and continued to rocket toward the hunters. He was going too fast to stop now. He crouched low on his skis, trying to make himself a smaller target. It wasn't much, but it was the best he could come up with on short notice.

Behind the gaping barrel of the revolver, a look of surprise and doubt grew in Pearson's eyes. He jerked the gun away at the last second and jumped out of Joe's path, crashing into one of the hunters. Both men tumbled to the ground. The other hunter spun around, still clutching his rifle. Joe slammed into him and knocked the weapon loose. It sailed through the air, flipping end over end, and finally crashed into the side of the rock. The gun went off with a loud boom, something whizzed past Joe's ear, and there was a sharp *spang* behind him of bullet hitting metal.

Joe's momentum pushed him past the hunters. The hounds, already frightened and confused, scattered in all directions as he plowed toward them. The cougar's lips curled back in one last snarl before he leapt into the air and disappeared.

Pearson picked himself up and shoved the revolver into a leather holster. He stormed over to Joe and grabbed him by the collar, lifting him off the ground. "Are you insane, or just brain-dead?" he growled, his face as red as his beard. "You almost got yourself killed."

He dropped Joe roughly and glared at him with raging eyes. "And if I had known you were going to mess up the hunt and be responsible for a hole in my new Sno-Cat, I *would* have pulled the trigger."

Joe peered around the wide man and saw a ragged blotch of bare metal on one of the snowmobiles, where the black paint had flaked off. "That's not exactly a hole," he observed, trying to sound cool and casual. "It's more like a severe dent."

"That's not the point!" the man roared. He gestured at the two bewildered hunters. "These gentlemen paid good money for a cougar hunt, and you just ruined the whole thing!"

Joe gazed at the man with steady eyes like

cold, blue ice. "What you were doing didn't have much to do with hunting."

"What's that supposed to mean?" the man demanded sharply.

Joe pointed at Frank, who was holding the arrow-shaped antenna over his head. At his feet was a metal box. A pointer on a numbered arc under a clear plastic cover on the top of the box danced as Frank waved the antenna around.

"It means you don't have to be much of a hunter to track mountain lions with this," Frank said. "You just have to be a mediocre meter reader."

"Do you boys have some problem with radio tracking gear?" the man snapped.

"Not when it's used for research," Joe responded. "K. D. Becker didn't put radio collars on those cats to make it easier for you to hunt them down."

The man pointed at the collar on one of the dogs, a thin wisp of wire jutting out from it. "Does that look like a cat to you? I use radio collars on my dogs to keep track of them. Sometimes they get too far ahead. Just about every cougar hunting guide uses them, and it's all perfectly legal.

"And did you actually *see* a collar on that cougar before you blundered in here?" he challenged.

Frank had been too far away, and he knew Joe would have been too busy to notice such details. "If you weren't tracking the cat electronically, how'd you find it so fast? You were out less than an hour."

The man shrugged his wide shoulders. "Just luck, I guess. There's no law against that, either."

Just then something flashed past the men. There was a metallic thunk, and the bearded man jumped backward as if he had been jabbed with an electric cattle prod. He was staring at the ground with a startled look on his face. Joe looked down and saw that the radio signal detector was now neatly skewered by a thin black arrow.

Ted Gentry stepped out from behind a nearby tree. There was already another steel-tipped arrow notched in his bow and pointed at the bearded man. "There may not be a law against luck, Pearson—but there *is* one against hunting on private property without permission.

"Besides, luck had nothing to do with it," he continued. "I heard a few stories about your amazing run of so-called luck and your quick kills. Something about it just didn't sound right." He glanced at Frank. "Nobody would ever accuse Mark Pearson of being a great hunter. So I decided to check it out."

His eyes shifted back to the bearded man. "I've been tailing you for the past three weeks. You took out three hunting parties and bagged three cougars. Two of the hunts lasted less than six hours, and both of those cats were wearing radio collars."

Pearson scowled. "That doesn't prove anything."

"No, it doesn't," Gentry admitted. "You've been pretty careful, and I wasn't sure until today."

"Wait a minute," one of the hunters interrupted. "The dogs never got out of sight, so he didn't even use the radio gear. He just turned it on at the start to make sure it was working."

"That's right," the other one joined in. "And we saw cougar tracks by the road and followed them here."

Gentry laughed. "You saw a few paw prints that didn't go anywhere. Pearson had already located the cat's den, probably sometime yesterday, judging by the snowmobile tracks I followed after I saw him making those fake cat tracks."

He nodded toward a rocky outcropping halfway up the side of the valley. "The cat was living in a small cave up there. All Pearson had to do was turn on the radio once to make sure he was home. And since Pearson was in the lead snowmobile, you never noticed that the only tracks he was following were his own."

Pearson glowered at Gentry. "Everybody knows you're crazy. I don't have to listen to any more of your babbling."

"You're free to leave any time," Gentry said.

"What are we waiting for?" one of the hunters complained. "There's a fresh set of tracks. We can still catch that cougar."

"That's right," Pearson replied, nodding his head firmly. "And that's exactly what we're going to do."

Gentry shook his head slowly. "I don't think so. As I said before, there's a law against hunting on private property without permission."

"That's between me and the owner," Pearson said gruffly. "And you're not the owner."

Gentry smiled. "I think we can safely assume that K. D. Becker didn't give you permission to hunt here, and she *is* the owner."

Pearson's only reply was a silent, stony stare. Finally he spun around and stomped back to his snowmobile, shouted a few terse commands, and the dogs scurried after him as he roared away. Once the two hunters realized what was happening, they hastily jumped on the other snowmobile and took off after him.

"Nice piece of detective work," Joe said as Gentry unnotched the arrow and snapped it back into the row of shafts in the miniquiver attached to the side of the bow. "Pearson must have found out which radio frequency Becker was using and adapted his equipment to tune into it."

"I don't understand people like that," Gentry said. "There's no honor in what he does, no dignity. He'd rather lie and cheat even when it's easier to be honest."

Frank looked at him closely. "He wasn't lying about seeing you that morning near the spot where Becker was shot, was he?"

Gentry didn't respond.

"You were there because you were following Pearson," Frank pressed.

Gentry nodded. "I was there."

"You should come into town with us and explain it to the sheriff," Joe said.

"No," Gentry replied after another pause. "You go back and tell the sheriff. I think I'll stay here in the mountains. This is where I belong."

He didn't say goodbye. He just turned and walked away.

Afternoon had faded to evening by the time Frank and Joe returned to town. Even though they were hungry and tired, they knew they had to see the sheriff before they did anything else. "Downtown" Elk Springs was only a single street lined with small stores and restaurants. At the end of the strip was a single-story brick building with one word on the sign above the door: Police.

The sheriff lumbered out the front door just as Frank and Joe were getting out of their car. "I was just talking about you boys a little while ago," he said in his country drawl.

"Is that good or bad?" Joe responded.

The sheriff chuckled. "Oh, pretty good, I

think. The young lady I was talking to had a fairly high opinion of you.'' He seemed to be enjoying some private joke.

"And who might that be?'' Frank asked. "I don't remember meeting any women in town.''

"You didn't meet her in town,'' the sheriff answered. "But you did run into her at work.''

Comprehension dawned on Joe's face. "You mean Becker's out of the coma? What did she say? Did she see the shooter? Is she all right? Can we see her?'' The words rushed out of his mouth in a rapid stream, the sentences strung together in one long question.

"Whoa,'' the sheriff cut in. "One at a time. Yes, she's out of the coma, and yes, she's talking. Well, it's more like meandering. She's not too coherent yet.''

"What about the shooting?'' Frank prodded. "Does she remember anything?''

"It's hard to say. Her dates are sort of mixed up right now.'' He paused and looked off in a distracted way, as if he were sorting out something in his mind. "Anyway, the doctor thinks she'll make a full recovery. All she needs is rest to give her body time to heal. If you boys are still in town tomorrow, you can visit her. I'm sure she'd like to thank you in person.''

"We'll still be here,'' Frank assured him.

Frank and Joe showed up at the hospital at exactly nine o'clock the next morning. Frank got a bad feeling when he saw the sheriff's jeep parked a few feet from the front entrance in an area clearly marked No Parking. Inside, they found the sheriff having a hushed conversation with a doctor and a nurse in the lobby.

The sheriff spotted the Hardys, said one last thing to the doctor, and strode across the lobby to intercept the two brothers. "I'm afraid K.D.'s had a little setback," he told them.

"What do you mean?" Frank asked. "What happened?"

The sheriff scratched his mustache. "She's been on a respirator ever since they operated on her to remove the bullet. She'd been having a little trouble breathing on her own."

"If she's been on a respirator the whole time," Joe said, "I wouldn't call it a setback."

"I was getting to that part," the sheriff replied. He pushed up the brim of his cowboy hat and stroked his mustache again. "Something went wrong with the respirator during the night. By the time the nurse discovered the problem, K.D. had slipped back into a coma."

Chapter 11

"THE SHERIFF should have put a guard on her room!" Joe muttered as they left the hospital.

"Sheriff Stevens has only two deputies," Frank reminded him. "And we don't know that the respirator problem wasn't an accident of some kind."

Joe stared at his brother. "You don't really believe that, do you?"

Frank hesitated. "Not really. As a general rule, I don't believe in tidy coincidences.'"

"So what do we do about it?"

"For the moment, nothing," Frank said. He turned up his collar against the cold wind as they walked to the car. "The sheriff's a fairly bright guy. I think he can check out this situation without our help."

"While we just sit around our motel and wait?" Joe responded in an abrasive tone. He yanked open the car door and slipped into the driver's seat.

"We could do that," Frank said mildly as he slid into the seat next to Joe. He gazed absently out the window at the clear sky. "I thought it might be a nice day for a drive, though."

Joe jammed the key into the ignition and gave it a sharp twist. The engine complained that it was too cold to start, but it started, anyway. "Any place in particular?" he asked, clutching the steering wheel in a two-fisted choke hold.

Frank shrugged. "We could take in the sights of the bustling metropolis of Elk Springs."

"That should take about five minutes," Joe muttered.

Frank smiled a secret smile. "That sounds about right."

Joe shot a sidelong glance at his brother. "What's going on in that mental computer of yours?"

"Just drive around until you find something that looks like a library," Frank said. "I'll tell you when we get there."

It didn't take long to find the small public library. Inside, a plump, smiling woman stood behind the check-out counter.

"May I help you?" she asked in a bright, cheerful voice.

The place was deserted, and Frank guessed that their visit was a welcome occurrence. That was good. It would make their job easier.

"I sure hope so," he said. He tried to sound both friendly and just a little distraught. "I've been to six libraries in three counties, and this is my last shot."

The woman's smile faltered. "Oh dear. We don't have a very big selection of books. What were you looking for?"

"I'm working on a term paper on historical land-use patterns," Frank explained. He leaned forward and spoke in a hushed tone. "If I don't get a good grade, I'll lose my table tennis scholarship."

The woman made an apologetic face. "I'm afraid all we have is a set of county land maps." She led him over to a table at the back of the room. "They go back about fifty years. They indicate the property owner's name only, not what the land is used for."

Frank tried to look disappointed. "Maybe I can find something out from them," he said somberly.

Actually, he couldn't believe their luck. The huge maps had a wealth of detail: property lines, title owners, locations of houses, even garages and barns.

"What are we looking for?" Joe asked, joining his brother after the woman went back to her desk.

"What do Becker and Gentry have in common?"

Joe studied his brother studying the most recent map, which was less than a year old. Then the answer came to him. "They both own land around here."

"Bingo," Frank replied. "And quite a lot of it, if this thing is accurate."

Joe frowned slightly. "What does that have to do with anything?"

"Dick Oberman said a new highway project might bring some new life into town," Frank answered. "If somebody wanted to make a big killing, he could buy real estate cheap now and then sell it for a big profit after the new highway makes the land more attractive to developers." He left the rest unsaid.

Joe filled in the blanks. "Then Becker and Gentry are perfect targets. Neither of them uses the land for ranching, and they both need money for their special causes."

Frank nodded. "What do you think would happen if neither of them wanted to sell?"

Joe smiled grimly. "It would be convenient if one of them killed the other one. With one dead and the other behind bars, somebody could probably buy up their land at bargain prices."

A troubled look passed over his face. "Of course, this is all speculation. With Becker in a coma and Gentry kind of on the run, we can't confirm any of this. We don't know if anybody tried to buy their land—much less who."

"For now, let's just assume that's the way it is," Frank suggested. "Now, who could really benefit from this? Maybe someone who already owns land that abuts theirs. It might make sense to be able to sell a really giant parcel of land—perhaps to a resort developer. Whose land borders on K.D.'s and Ted's?" he asked.

Joe looked down. His brother's finger was running back and forth across the map. He stopped it on the words Lazy W Ranch—Owner: W. Crawford.

"So far, this is all guesswork," Joe pointed out as he steered the car toward the Lazy W.

"That's why we have to check it out on our own and not involve the sheriff yet," Frank replied.

"How are we going to get Crawford to talk to us?" Joe asked as he pulled up next to the main gate of the ranch.

Frank patted a large manila envelope on his lap. It had taken two dollars' worth of quarters and a considerable amount of jockeying with the oversize sheet of paper to make a complete photocopy of the map, but he had succeeded. "Let me handle this," he said. He rolled down his window and beamed at the cowboy sentry. "We have some important papers here for Mr. Crawford," he announced.

The cowboy hunched over and squinted in at

the envelope Frank was waving around. "What kind of papers?"

"How should I know?" Frank responded. "They only pay us to deliver the stuff. All I know is that if the package is marked Urgent, we're supposed to make sure it gets there the same day." He stuck the envelope in the man's face. "See? Right there."

The cowboy pulled back his head and eyed the hand-scrawled red letters. "This doesn't look very official," he remarked doubtfully.

"That's because it's urgent," Frank said. "There wasn't time to make it look pretty."

"All right," the sentry said, reaching out for the envelope. "Give it to me."

Frank held the envelope clutched tight to his chest. "No way. I have to deliver this personally."

"I can't let you in without clearance," the sentry told him.

Frank smiled. "That's okay. We can wait. It's all part of the service. And maybe you'll get some kind of bonus for holding up the delivery of these *urgent* papers."

The man started to scowl, caught himself, and turned it into a resigned shrug. "Aw, what do I care? I signed on to be a cowboy, not a guard dog. I'll just let 'em know you're coming." He trudged over to the small guard house and disappeared inside. A few seconds later the iron gate swung open.

Joe drove up to the big main house and parked. As they walked up the front steps, Walt Crawford came storming out onto the porch. "What's all this about ur—" he started to shout and then cut himself off when he saw the Hardys. "Not you two again. What do you want now?"

"Just a few minutes of your time," Frank said pleasantly. "That's all."

Crawford stood at the top of the steps, staring down at them. "Go ahead, I'm listening."

"Out here?" Joe asked with a shiver, stuffing his hands in his coat pockets.

Crawford nodded. "That's right." Even with no coat, he seemed unaware of the extreme cold.

"I can understand why you might be upset," Frank said. "We thought you should know what we found out."

Crawford arched his eyebrows but didn't say anything.

Frank took a deep breath and plunged in with both feet. "We believe that Ted Gentry is being framed for the shooting of K. D. Becker."

Crawford's hard eyes flicked to the envelope in Frank's hand. "What's in there? Evidence?"

"Evidence that somebody wanted them both out of the way," Frank said evenly.

"I see," Crawford responded in a guarded tone. "And who would want to do that?"

"You know who and why!" Joe blurted out.

"With their land combined with what you already own, developers would be throwing money at you once the new highway is finished."

A smug smile spread across Crawford's face. "I have no interest in their property, and I have even less interest in developers. In fact, I've spent a lot of time and money fighting that highway bill."

Joe scowled. "Why?"

"Because I'm in the cattle ranching business," Crawford replied in a calm voice, like a parent patiently lecturing a child. "And it's a good business. If somebody decides to build a resort or hotels next door, my property taxes will skyrocket, and that will eat up most of my profits. That's bad business."

He glanced at an expensive gold watch on his wrist. "Your few minutes are up. Now, get out of here before I have you arrested for trespassing."

"We sure were terrific," Joe grumbled loudly as they drove past the front gate. He gave the steering wheel a hard jerk, and the car swerved out onto the road.

Frank gazed out the window at the cattle and bales of hay that dotted the rolling fields of snow. "The plan was to draw him into a conversation and see if anything slipped out, not hurl accusations in his face."

A sign flashed by outside the window. Frank

kept staring out at the cattle. Something clicked in his head. He sat up stiffly and twisted around. "Stop the car," he said sharply.

Joe glanced over at him. "What?"

"Stop the car and back up," Frank said in a firm, insistent tone.

"Whatever you say," Joe muttered, putting his foot on the brake and shifting into reverse.

When they were past the signpost again, Frank told his brother to stop. He pointed at the sign. "What's wrong with this picture?"

" 'Welcome to Gunnison National Forest,' " Joe said, reading the words out loud. "What's wrong with that?"

Frank jerked his thumb over his shoulder. "Crawford's ranch is there—this is the border between his land and the national forest."

Joe gave him a blank look. "I still don't see what's wrong."

Frank gestured at the cattle on the gentle hills in front of them. "Crawford's cattle are on the wrong side of the sign. They're grazing in the national forest—the same national forest that K. D. Becker wants to turn into a wildlife refuge."

Chapter 12

JOE REACHED OUT and put his hand on his brother's shoulder. "I don't know how to tell you this," he said in a solemn voice, "but cows can't read."

Frank continued to stare straight ahead.

"Don't you think some official person would try to stop them from eating government property?" Joe asked.

Frank was silent for another minute. "Not if there was a lease," he finally said.

"Could you rewind that and play it for me again?" Joe responded in a puzzled voice.

"It's possible to lease parts of national forests," Frank explained. "That's part of what makes them different from national parks. Oil and lumber companies do it all the time."

"And cattle ranchers, too," Joe ventured. "Crawford gets some low-rent grazing land, and the government makes a little money. Everybody comes out ahead."

"Until K. D. Becker comes along with different plans for this part of the national forest," Frank said, filling in the next step.

Joe nodded. "I don't think steers count as wildlife. That means Crawford would have a lot to lose if Becker is successful."

"And if Gentry's people get the land," Frank added, "Crawford still loses. Getting rid of Becker and Gentry might not solve his problems, but it would buy him time."

"Crawford was out of town when Becker was shot," Joe recalled. "But he could have hired somebody to do the job for him. That won't be easy to prove."

Frank drummed his fingers on the dashboard. "We have to link him to the shooter somehow," he said half out loud. "If we had any idea who actually did the shooting, we might be able to put something together. Since we don't, we just have to wait to see if Crawford makes a move. Maybe we rattled him today. If we get lucky and he doesn't just call, he might lead us right to the trigger man."

Joe let out a low groan. "Does that mean what I think it means?"

Frank put on an innocent face. "I don't know. What do you think it means?"

"Stakeout," Joe muttered.

"Bingo," Frank replied with a smile. "There was a little side road about fifty yards from the main gate. We should be able to keep an eye on everything that comes in and out from there."

"Let's go back to town and get something to eat first," Joe suggested hopefully. "By the time we get back, it'll be dark. Nobody will spot us as long as we keep the headlights off."

Frank shook his head. "We can't take the chance. We might miss something important."

Joe sighed. "How long do we hang around and wait?"

Frank shrugged. "If nothing happens by midnight, we'll reconsider our options."

They didn't have to wait that long. The sun had barely slipped behind the jagged mountain peaks, when the gate swung open and a car pulled out. There was still enough light lingering in the sky to give Joe a good look at the driver.

He nudged his brother and switched on the engine. "There goes Crawford. If this trail leads to a restaurant, I'm going to follow him all the way inside, grab a table, and order some dinner. And if he leaves before I'm finished, he's on his own."

"He's going the wrong way for that," Frank said. "Elk Springs is in the opposite direction. The way he's headed, the road climbs into the mountains. That's a good sign."

"Why is it a good sign?" Joe asked, frowning.

"If Crawford is meeting the person he hired to shoot Becker and frame Gentry," Frank began, "he wouldn't want to be seen with the guy in broad daylight, not in town or at the ranch. He'd pick an out-of-the-way meeting place."

Joe turned on the headlights. "And he'd do it at night, under cover of darkness. Don't forget that part."

Frank smiled. "If I do, I'm sure you'll remind me." He reached over and switched off the headlights. "Just like I'll remind you not to shoot off any flares or fireworks to let Crawford know we're behind him. Keep him on a short leash and let him light the way."

That trick worked fairly well until the road got treacherous, hugging the side of a peak that disappeared into darkness and snaking steadily upward with sharp twists and turns. Joe hoped they wouldn't hit an icy patch and wipe out. Every time the lead car disappeared around a blind curve, the glow from its headlights vanished, too, and Joe had to flick on his own beams to pierce the blackness that swallowed the next treacherous turn. Halfway around the bend, he'd switch them off again. It was all a matter of timing. If he didn't turn them off fast enough, Crawford would spot them. If he didn't turn them *on* fast enough, he might miss the turn.

Frank was studying the road just as intently as his brother. Up ahead, the mountainside jutted outward, and he could clearly see the wide beams of Crawford's headlights moving toward another hairpin turn.

This one was slightly different from the others. It had a wide shoulder and a wooden guard rail. Frank caught a glimpse of what might have been benches facing out over the ledge, and he realized that there was some sort of scenic overlook. That wasn't all he glimpsed.

"Whoa," he said in a low voice, as if somebody might overhear him. "Looks like we just hit the jackpot."

Joe stopped the car and killed the engine. "Either that," he whispered, "or it's another one of those tidy coincidences that you hate so much."

The twin beams of Crawford's headlights lit up the blue metal of a battered pickup truck parked on the shoulder. The car pulled up next to the truck and stopped. Frank got out his monocular and managed to focus it on the scene just as a bulky figure stepped out of the truck. He wasn't surprised to see the red beard of Pearson.

The passenger-side door of Crawford's car swung open. The large, bearded man hesitated for a moment and then got in.

"What's going on?" Joe asked. "What are they doing?"

"I can't see inside the car," Frank answered. "It's too dark. It doesn't look like they're going anywhere, so it's a fairly solid bet Crawford and Pearson are having a little chat."

Joe snorted. "I doubt if they're planning a hunting trip, unless they're after more two-legged victims."

"If we don't want to end up on their itinerary," Frank said, "we'd better get out of here."

Joe twisted his head around and peered out the rear window. There was no room to turn around, and he couldn't risk turning on the engine. If Crawford or Pearson heard the noise and spotted the car, things might get a little rough.

There was only one way to go. He took a deep breath, released the emergency brake, and let the car roll slowly backward. The cloud cover had lifted and there was just enough light from the moon to outline the first bend behind him. Joe guided the car around it and stopped on the thin shoulder, just out of sight of the overlook.

He turned the key in the ignition and winced as the engine roared in the empty silence. He made a quick, tight U-turn in the narrow space, and headed back down the mountain. Thirty seconds later he managed to hear himself think over the pounding of his heart and remembered to turn on the headlights.

Frank peered out the window. "If you see anything like a side road, take it."

"Coming right up," Joe said. He knew what his brother had in mind. He slowed when he passed a narrow, dark lane. He backed the car into it, drove about twenty feet into the shadows, stopped, and killed the lights.

Then they waited.

Fifteen minutes later, Crawford's car went by. Joe put his foot on the gas pedal and the car rolled forward.

Frank reached out and touched his brother's arm. "Not yet. We got what we wanted from Crawford."

Five more minutes ticked by before the blue pickup truck shot past.

Joe let out a low whistle. "He must be doing at least fifty. That's really pushing it on this road. He must be in a hurry to get someplace."

"Let's find out where and why," Frank said.

"It's about time," Joe replied. He stepped on the gas and took off after the truck.

Joe didn't spend a lot of time worrying about being spotted. It took all his concentration to match the truck's breakneck pace and keep the car on the twisting roadway. A small patch of ice could send them over the edge. "If he's trying to shake us," he observed in a tight voice, "he's doing a good job."

Joe's hands were locked tightly on the steering wheel. His right foot jumped back and forth between the brake and gas pedals as the car screeched around each deadly curve. Joe knew that a thousand feet below, at the bottom of black nothingness, the cold, hard ground waited to embrace them.

Frank kept his eyes on the pickup truck. On the last turn, the outside tires had kicked up snow and gravel from the shoulder. It took the next turn even wider, and the tires kissed the edge of the cliff.

Frank glanced over at the speedometer. The needle was pushing sixty. "He's not trying to shake us," he said with grim certainty. "That truck's out of control—he can't slow it down."

Joe gritted his teeth and pressed down on the gas pedal. "Then we'll have to do it for him. I'll get in front of him so he can keep his front bumper against our rear one. Slowly I'll ease off on the gas and apply the brake. That should stop him."

Joe's foot didn't even touch the brake pedal on the next turn. The tires screamed and the back end fishtailed wildly. Joe did manage to keep the car on the pavement. He was even starting to gain on the truck, but not fast enough. He pushed down on the gas pedal again.

The car rocketed down a short straightaway, chewing up the distance. When he was close enough to read Pearson's license plate, he swerved into the outside lane and jammed the gas pedal all the way to the floor.

Even though the speedometer hovered at seventy, the side of the pickup truck seemed to crawl by in slow motion. A yellow warning sign with a curved black arrow symbol flashed past. Frank got a good look at Pearson's frantic, terrified face as the car nosed past the truck. Joe jerked the wheel, cut in front of the truck, and stomped on the brakes. Because of the curve he couldn't afford to ease Pearson's speed down slowly. He had to do it fast.

The tires screeched in protest. The pickup truck slammed into the rear end of the car. Frank's head snapped back as they lurched forward, but his eyes remained locked on what loomed ahead, framed in the harsh glare of the headlights.

The pavement disappeared as the road veered off to the right. The snow on the thin shoulder took on an ugly tinge in the yellow beams. Beyond that, the lights couldn't find anything and just dwindled away.

Frank's fingers sank deep into the armrest on the door as the heavy truck's momentum pushed them closer to the edge. "We're not going to make it!" he yelled. "We're going over!"

Chapter 13

METAL GROANED and rubber smoked as the runaway truck bulldozed the car closer to the edge of the cliff. Joe threw all his strength against the brake pedal, but he couldn't outmuscle the laws of physics. The pickup truck had too much weight and too much momentum. He couldn't stop it from going over the edge. If he didn't do something fast, they'd go down with it.

Joe grappled the steering wheel, cranking it away from the cliff. If he could have pried his hands off the wheel, he might have crossed his fingers. Since he couldn't, he just swallowed hard and did what he had to do.

He yanked his foot off the brake and hit the gas. The car shot forward, away from the overpowering mass of the doomed truck. The back end swung out, and the left rear tire skidded across the snowy shoulder, flirting briefly with the empty darkness beyond. Then the front tires grabbed the snow-covered road and the car swerved around the curve.

Frank looked back and saw the pickup truck desperately trying to follow. It did a half-spin, slid sideways to the edge of the precipice, hung there for a second, and then tumbled into the black void.

Joe braked to a stop, and they both jumped out and ran back up the road to the spot where the truck had gone over. Frank didn't really expect to see much in the deep darkness. So it was quite a jolt when he peered over the edge and saw blazing headlights only about sixty feet below. There was a ledge with two scraggly, twisted pines jutting out of it. The truck was wedged precariously between the trees and the rocky cliff, half off the ledge.

"Hello!" Frank shouted. "Can you hear me down there?"

There was no response and no movement from the truck.

Frank glanced over at his brother. "There's a rope in my pack."

"Not for long," Joe said. He dashed down the road and came back with more than the rope. He brought the car, too.

Joe lashed one end of the rope to the front bumper while Frank looped the other end around his chest. When they were both ready, Joe stood at the edge of the cliff, gripping the rope with both hands. He let out the line a handful at a time so Frank could rappel down the rocky slope.

His feet scrabbled over huge boulders, loose rocks, and pebbles that clattered down into the darkness. Some of them clanked and thunked off the hood and roof of the stranded truck. Frank angled down into the open cargo bed behind the cab. The scrawny trees creaked and swayed. The truck rocked ominously.

He could see Pearson inside the cab, slumped over the steering wheel. Frank hoped he was only unconscious. Using a fist-size rock, he smashed out the glass and then cleared away the jagged shards with his gloved hands.

He leaned into the cab and grabbed Pearson's shoulders. The truck groaned and nosed down sharply. Frank quickly hauled the heavy, limp body out of the cab, and the truck tilted back again.

"Are you all right?" Joe called down.

"Yeah!" Frank shouted up. "For now, anyway. One wrong move, and this truck could go over. You're going to have to pull us up together, and this guy is heavy. He must weigh over two fifty."

"No problem," Joe replied. "I've got a friend here who must weigh a couple *thousand* pounds. Hang on! We'll have you up in a minute."

Joe ran over to the car and took out the floor mats. He lifted up the slack rope, draped the mats over the rough edge of the cliff, and laid the rope back down on top of the layer of protective padding. He knew the mats would keep the rope from fraying. Then he went back to the car, hopped into the driver's seat, started the engine, and backed up slowly.

His head swiveled back and forth between the pavement behind him and the taut rope in front. When he saw Frank's head poke above the cliff, Joe stopped the car, jumped out, and ran over to help his brother wrestle the massive red-bearded man onto the shoulder of the road.

Pearson was still alive. There was an ugly purple lump on his forehead, and he was out cold, but he was still breathing. They loaded him into the backseat and headed down the mountain.

Pearson was still unconscious when a doctor and nurse wheeled him off on a gurney at Elk Springs Hospital. Frank and Joe were about to leave the emergency room, when Sheriff Stevens lumbered in.

"News sure does travel fast in a small town," Joe commented. "We were just about to call you."

"I was already here when I got word you boys had brought in another body," the sheriff said. "As long as you're in town, maybe I should just move my office in here. It would probably save a lot of time and bother."

"Were you here on police business?" Frank asked. "Or was it just a social call?"

The sheriff smiled. "A little bit of both. I came over to have a chat with K.D."

"She's awake?" Joe asked eagerly. "Can we see her?"

"I think that can be arranged," the sheriff said, "even though it's after visiting hours. But first, I think you have to fill me in on what hit Mark Pearson and how you fit into it."

The Hardys told him what happened, and the sheriff listened quietly, nodding occasionally. After Joe described how they saved Pearson, Stevens just sat and let the facts sink in.

"I suppose you boys have a theory about all this," he finally said in a relaxed tone.

"What we guess happened is that Crawford hired Pearson to kill Becker. He must have decided that Pearson would go along with it because the wildlife refuge would ruin his hunting business. Then Crawford must have decided to get rid of Pearson."

"And why would he do that—according to your theory, that is?" the sheriff asked softly.

Joe shrugged. "Maybe he got nervous. Maybe Pearson wanted more money, or maybe Crawford just decided he was unreliable. So Crawford asked Pearson to meet him out on a remote mountain road. Then someone, somehow, got under Pearson's truck and cut his brake line."

"Did you hear what Crawford and Pearson talked about?" the sheriff asked.

"No," Joe admitted.

"You think it was one of Crawford's men who tampered with Pearson's brakes?" the sheriff asked.

The boys nodded.

"Did you *see* anyone crawl under Pearson's truck?"

"There was a thick cloud cover," Frank pointed out, "and we weren't watching the whole time, so we didn't see anyone."

"But don't you think Pearson would have seen something? And where did this man come from?" the sheriff questioned, not buying into their theory.

"If Crawford set up the meeting," Frank answered, "he could have sent out a man ahead of time." He paused and ran it over in his mind. "The man could have parked up the road and out of sight, backtracked on foot, and then hid until they arrived."

"If you can pull the truck back onto the road, it should be easy enough to check the brake lines to see if they've been cut," Frank suggested.

Stevens looked at his watch. "It's getting late. If you boys want to have a word with K.D. you'd better do it now," he said, dismissing them and their theory.

A hospital aide directed Frank and Joe to Becker's room. She was propped up in bed, and a nurse was drawing blood from her arm. She was pale but alert and smiled weakly when she saw the Hardys.

"Isn't that just like a hospital?" Joe cracked after the nurse left. "If you're not dead when you get to one, they bleed you to death a teaspoon at a time."

Becker laughed softly. "Are you saying I'd be out of here by now if they didn't keep stealing my blood. Of course, I might have a lot less to steal if you guys hadn't come along when you did. At least, that's what they tell me. I can't remember anything that happened that day."

"You don't remember getting up or having breakfast?" Joe asked.

"Oh, sure, I remember breaking camp and coming back to the canyon. Everything after that is a complete blank, though."

"You came back to the canyon?" Frank responded. "What do you mean? You didn't camp there?"

Becker shook her head. "I camped a few miles farther up in the hills. In the morning, I picked up a new signal on the radio, which led me back to the canyon." She paused, frowning slightly. "According to the meter, the signal source shouldn't have been more than ten feet away, but I didn't see any sign of a cat in the canyon, and the snow had let up right then, so I shouldn't have missed it."

"What time was that?" Frank asked.

"About nine-fifteen," she replied. "I know because I wrote it down in my log book."

"Your watch was broken at ten forty-six," Joe said. "That leaves an hour and a half unaccounted for."

Becker frowned again. "I know. The doctor told me amnesia isn't unusual in severe trauma cases, but it's driving me crazy. I can't figure out what I did there all that time."

"Speaking of time," Frank said, "it's late. We should let you get some rest."

Becker sighed. "I guess so. They tell me that's the only way I'll get out of here." She closed her eyes. "Come back and see me tomorrow."

"It's a date," Frank said over his shoulder as he stepped into the hallway. He was surprised to see Sheriff Stevens leaning against the wall outside the door.

"Do you solve a lot of cases by eavesdropping?" Frank asked coolly.

"A fair number," the sheriff responded. "I had one of my men drive out to take a look at the crash site. He just radioed back to me that that's a dangerous rockslide area. A man could get killed just trying to hook on a tow hitch. I'm not going to order anybody to do it, and I don't think I'm going to find too many volunteers. We have to leave the truck where it is."

* * *

The next morning Frank and Joe were standing on the edge of the road, looking down at the wreck of the pickup truck.

There was a wide ledge about twenty feet below the one the truck had crashed onto. The truck had shifted during the night, and the front end now tilted down at an even sharper angle.

"It could go over any minute," Joe said. "You'll have to put some weight in the back and try to balance the thing while I go under and check the brake line."

"Right idea," Frank replied. "Wrong job assignments. If anybody's going to crawl around under there, it's going to be me." Joe didn't argue.

Tying a rope to their car bumper again, they used it to secure themselves as they worked their way down to the truck. Joe let go of the rope and stepped into the cargo bed. Metal creaked and the truck rocked back a few inches. Frank tried to peer under it.

He was about to tell Joe to shift his weight farther back in the bed, when he felt the side of the cliff tremble and heard a low rumble from above.

Frank raised his head just in time to see an avalanche of rocks and boulders crashing down toward them.

Chapter 14

A GIANT BOULDER cartwheeled down the slope, barely missing the front fender of the pickup. There were more on the way.

Frank jerked open the door of the cab and dove in. He had tossed the rope to Joe who scrambled in behind him. With their extra weight, the truck pitched down at a dizzying angle. Rocks hammered onto the roof with a deafening din. A huge boulder smashed into the cargo bed, and luckily the front end lurched up again.

"What do we do?" Joe cried out, swallowing hard to fight down the sick feeling in his stomach.

Frank snatched up the shoulder harness from behind him and hauled it roughly across his chest. "Buckle up!" he yelled.

"I don't think that's going to help much!" Joe

shouted as he slammed the buckle into the slot. Something crashed into the roof, leaving a fist-shaped dent next to his head.

"It couldn't hurt!" Frank screamed over the roaring tide of earth and stone and snow.

A rock shattered the windshield, which was now a maze of tiny cracks. There was a groaning, rending noise. The stunted trees jerked and shuddered as the ledge they had clung to crumbled away. The force of the landslide and the weight of the truck were too much for their root systems. They lost their tenuous grasp, and joined the rocks in their race to the bottom. The truck joined in, too.

Joe felt the world drop out from under him, and his stomach jumped into his throat. Then everything spun around in confusion. He had just enough time to figure out that the truck had flipped over before a searing jolt of pain brought an abrupt halt to all his figuring.

Joe woke up with a sharp ache in his neck and a dull throb across his chest. He coughed and gagged on the thick dust swirling around him. "Well, that's a good sign," he groaned. "I'm still breathing." Peering through the dim haze, he could see that he was still in the truck. Thin shafts of sunlight trickled in through the rocky debris and dirty snow that iced the crumpled cab. Joe was dangling upside down in the shoulder harness, the straps biting into his skin, his head wedged against the ceiling.

"We're lucky to be alive," Frank said in a hoarse whisper.

Joe tried to laugh. "You call this living?"

Frank thumbed the release button on his shoulder harness and slowly slid down onto the ceiling. He moved his arms and legs carefully, one at a time, then clenched and opened his fists. He swiveled his head from side to side. "Nothing broken. How about you?"

Joe unbuckled himself and joined his brother in the cramped space. "I'm okay, but I don't think anybody will be driving this heap anywhere for quite a while.

"And that brings up an interesting question," he continued. "Why aren't we dead? We should be buried under several thousand tons of rubble at the losing end of a very long drop."

"That's where the luck comes in," Frank explained. "I think the truck plowed into that ledge that was twenty feet below where we were. Something pinned us here while the rockslide rumbled past."

"That's a great theory," Joe replied. "Let's see if we can test it."

He turned himself around in the tight space and faced the door. He tugged on the handle and pushed. Rocks and dirt shifted. More sunlight streamed in. The door opened a crack but wouldn't budge any farther. Joe tried jiggling it back and forth. The rocks moved some more, and a little more light seeped in. The opening was now wide enough for a scrawny, greased cat.

Joe rocked back on his hands and knees, tucked his head down, and slammed his shoulder into the door. Dirt and stones fell away, light flooded in, and the door flew open. Joe toppled forward into clear blue, empty air. He flailed his arms wildly and snagged the door handle with one hand.

He hung there for a few seconds like a human bridge, his toes in the cab, hooked around the rim of the doorway, and one arm stretched across the gulf to the handle of the wide-open door. He stared down in wide-eyed surprise. A bird glided in lazy circles some distance below him. Joe guessed that the distance between him and the bird was about the length of a football field. Another football field below the bird was the base of the cliff.

"Well, your theory passed the first test," Joe remarked after his brother hauled him back inside.

He poked his head out cautiously and looked around. The half-buried truck was less than a foot from the edge of the ledge. He twisted around, grasped the metal running board with both hands, and lifted himself out and onto the bottom of the wreck.

"What about the brakes," Frank asked after Joe helped him out.

Joe gestured at the twisted wreckage. "I don't think they work anymore."

Frank nodded ruefully. "Any signs of tampering were probably destroyed in that landslide."

Joe had brushed away some debris and found the tattered end of their rope. "At least we haven't run out of luck completely."

He tugged on it, and a section of line popped out of the loose layer of dust and small rocks. He gave it another tug and more rope appeared, leading straight up the slope, all the way to the road above. He put all his weight behind one final pull to make sure the line was secure.

He turned to Frank with a wide grin. "Never let anyone accuse the Hardy brothers of buying cheap climbing gear."

The sun was high in the sky when the Hardys drove back into Elk Springs. They wanted to find out about Pearson's condition and have another talk with K. D. Becker, so they made the hospital their first stop.

Frank pushed through the revolving door into the lobby and limped toward the front desk. He winced slightly, trying to ignore a throbbing pain in his left leg.

An orderly rushed over with a wheelchair. "Don't worry," he said in a way that immediately made Frank worry. "We'll get you down to the emergency room, and a doctor will fix you right up." He tried to push Frank into the chair.

Frank waved him off. "There's nothing wrong wi—" He caught a glimpse of his reflection in the spotless, shiny tile floor. He looked down at himself. His pants were ripped in a dozen places. His red down vest had turned dull gray with a thick coat of rock dust. He didn't want to think about the condition of his face and hair. He glanced over at his brother. Joe's thick blond hair was doing an imitation of a dirty brown dust mop. The right sleeve of his coat was torn half-way off at the shoulder.

A grin crossed Joe's grimy face. "You look like you've been playing football in a war zone," he said.

Frank smiled. "So do you." He turned back to the puzzled orderly. "We're okay. Really."

"Yeah," Joe said. "We're just slobs. Is there someplace where we can clean up?"

The orderly gestured vaguely down the hall to a public washroom and wandered off. The Hardys did their best to make themselves presentable. The result weren't pretty, but at least they didn't resemble the living dead anymore.

"We forgot to get visitors' passes," Frank remembered as they walked down the corridor. Doctors and nurses hustled back and forth and bustled in and out of rooms. Nobody stopped the Hardys.

"The halls at Bayport High are more tightly secured than this place," Joe commented.

Frank knocked softly on Becker's door. The door swung open, and he found himself face-to-face with Dick Oberman.

"Oh, hi," Frank said. "I'm sorry. We didn't know you were here."

Oberman motioned them inside. "Come on in. I was just leaving anyway, and K.D. could use the company."

"I sure could," Becker called out from her bed. "This place is boring!"

Oberman glanced at his watch. "Well, I'd better get going. I told my clerk I'd be at the store at ten, and it's almost noon."

"Why didn't you say something earlier?" Becker responded. "You didn't have to sit with me all this time."

He turned and smiled at her. "If you think *this* is boring, you should try retail sales sometime. I'm always finding excuses not to work. In fact, if I hadn't planned on visiting you this morning, I probably would have blown off the whole day and gone skiing instead."

That triggered something in Frank's mind. "What about the day K.D. was shot? Did you go skiing that morning?"

Oberman's cold blue eyes narrowed. "Why do you ask?"

Frank studied him carefully, curious at his reaction. "No special reason. I just thought you might have seen something to help break the case, that's all."

Oberman relaxed visibly. "Oh, of course. I'm afraid I can't help you out there. I was at the store at eleven sharp that morning. I had to be there to receive a shipment of goods."

He moved to the door. "I really have to run. I'll try to stop back again tonight, K.D."

"Not many people have close friends like that," Joe remarked after Oberman left.

Becker gave him a strange look. "What do you mean?"

"Uh, nothing," Joe replied, somewhat flustered. "It's just that it seemed like he spent all his spare time at your bedside while you were in the coma. I guess I just assumed the two of you were pretty tight."

Becker shook her head slowly. "I've known Dick a long time, but I've hardly seen him the past couple of years. I guess you could say we're still friends, but we were never close."

Frank's eyes roved around the room. "We brought your gear in with us when we carried you down from the mountain. Do you know what happened to your backpack?"

"Sure," Becker said. "It's in the closet over in the corner. I hope all my equipment is there. I haven't checked." She held up an arm with an IV tube strapped to it. "I've been sort of tied up."

Frank got out the backpack and quickly found

what he was looking for. He held up the small metal cylinder with the stubby antenna. "We found this near the spot where you were shot and put it in here. Is this one of your radio transmitters?"

Becker studied the object for a moment. "This is similar to the transmitters I used six or seven years ago, but it's not one of mine."

Joe responded with a perplexed frown. "If you didn't lose it, who did?"

Chapter 15

FRANK PULLED a chair over to the bed and sat down heavily. He stared at K. D. Becker for a long moment. The narrow escape from the rock-slide that morning really had taken its toll on his body, and the twists and turns in this case were giving his brain the same battered and bruised feeling.

"Oberman mentioned that he used to help you with your research," he finally said. "How much does he know about your radio telemetry equipment?"

"It would be easier to tell you what he *doesn't* know," Becker answered. "Back in the days when Dick was involved, I was making my own transmitter collars. He did a lot of that work. He probably could have been a real electronics whiz if he'd stuck with it. I guess he was more interested in sports."

Frank held up the device. "Do you think he could still build a transmitter?"

Becker shrugged. "Probably. I don't know why he'd want to, though. What would he use it for?"

Frank pushed himself out of the chair. "I'm not sure. Maybe we can find out." He stopped in the doorway and turned around. "I almost forgot. Have you heard anything about Mark Pearson's condition?"

"He had to have some kind of emergency surgery last night," Becker said. "The nurse I asked didn't have too many specifics. He's probably still in recovery."

"I guess that rules out bursting into his room and grilling him relentlessly for hours," Joe remarked.

Frank shot a look at his brother. "You've been reading too many cheap detective novels."

"They don't come much cheaper than us," Joe replied.

A few minutes and a short drive later, the Hardys were back at the Elk Springs Public Library.

"I don't think we're going to find a section on former Olympic hopefuls in here," Joe said as Frank pulled up to the curb and parked.

"What we're looking for isn't in a book," Frank replied.

"Then why are we wasting time at the library?"

Frank turned to his brother and smiled. "Trust me. I have a plan."

Joe rolled his eyes upward and groaned softly. "*Your* plans always get *me* in trouble."

"What kind of trouble can you get into in a library?"

Joe eyed him warily. "I don't know, and I'm not eager to find out."

Frank opened his door and got out of the car. "Have it your way. Stay here while I go inside."

"Really?"

"Really." Frank started to shut the door, paused, and stuck his head back inside. "Just one little thing."

"I knew it," Joe muttered. "What?"

"Wait ten minutes, and then come in and distract the librarian for me."

"Why?"

"Trust me. I have a pl—"

"I know, I know," Joe interrupted. "Take your plan and get going."

Frank walked into the library and found the librarian behind the counter again.

"Did you finish your report?" she asked.

"I'm afraid not," Frank said in a glum tone. "I need to get some more data somewhere. I don't even know where to start. Not that it matters. There's not enough time to go anywhere else."

"Well, if you let me know what you're looking

for, perhaps I could help you somehow," the librarian said.

"Maybe you can," Frank said. "Do you have an interlibrary lending service?"

The librarian's face lit up. "Why, yes, we do. It's a brand-new computerized system, too. I'm still learning how to use it."

Frank smiled. "Maybe *I* can help *you*. Where's the computer?"

She took him to a small office in the back of the library. The personal computer on the desk was a fairly recent model. Frank gave the setup a quick scan before he hit the power switch and sat down at the keyboard.

"Does it have an internal modem?" he asked as the machine started to hum and light flickered on the monitor screen."

"I have no idea," the woman said cheerfully. "They told me it was user-friendly, whatever that means. I don't know anything about how it works."

Frank looked at her with patient eyes. "Is it connected to the phone lines?"

"Oh, yes. Well, it has to be, doesn't it? I mean, how else would it talk to the computers at the other libraries?"

"So you just turn it on, type in some commands, and you're hooked up to the network, right?"

The librarian frowned. "Commands? I just use

the mouse gadget to point at what I want on the screen."

Frank looked at the colorful digital version of a desktop glowing on the monitor. It was filled with computerized images of tiny file folders. Inside each folder, Frank knew, there were software programs and data files. He moved the mouse and a pointer on the screen moved the same direction. When the pointer was on a folder marked Telecom, Frank clicked the mouse button.

"Where's the murder mystery section?" a loud voice bellowed from the library. "Doesn't anybody work here?"

The librarian glanced around nervously. "Oh my. I should go see what that man wants."

"Go ahead," Frank said as he studied the contents of the electronic folder. "I'll be fine."

"But I haven't even told you how to—"

"Don't worry," Frank cut in. "I'm sure I can figure it out." In fact, he already had. All he needed now was a little time and a little privacy, and he hoped Joe's little diversion would give him both.

"I can't figure out these numbers at all!" the irate voice complained loudly. "What ever happened to the Dewey decimal system anyway? Why don't they just put the dumb things in alphabetical order?"

The librarian wavered in the doorway. "Are you sure—"

"Yes, yes," Frank assured her. "It sounds like he needs your help more than I do." Frank hoped the librarian didn't recognize Joe. Joe had stayed in the background on their last visit—maybe she wouldn't remember him.

Joe was waiting in the car with a stack of faded, dog-eared whodunits in his lap when Frank came out of the library.

"I now have an Elk Springs Library card that's good for the next three years," Joe said. "What did you get?"

"Nothing that impressive," Frank replied with a grin. "Just the lowdown on the finances of a certain camping supply store owner."

Joe raised his eyebrows. "I didn't know they had a section in the library for that kind of information."

"They don't. I used their computer to link up with our computer at home."

"I didn't know *we* had that kind of information, either," Joe remarked.

"We don't," Frank replied. "But we do have a file on the hard disk memory with telephone numbers and access codes for various electronic bulletin boards, data retrieval systems, and a few credit record services."

"I get it now," Joe said. "You ran a credit check on Dick Oberman." He paused and a puzzled look crossed his face. "What I don't get is why."

"There are many motives for murder," Frank explained. "Money is one of the top ten."

"Is that what you found out from the computer?" Joe asked doubtfully.

"No," Frank said. "I found out that Oberman doesn't have any big debts, not anymore, anyway."

"I'm tired and hungry and my feet hurt," Joe complained. "Could you just hit me with the punchline instead of dangling it over my head?"

"Dick Oberman was in deep debt," Frank revealed. "His combined total credit card debt was over forty thousand dollars. Then, all of a sudden, he has a clean slate—everything paid in full."

Joe held up his hand before Frank could finish. "Don't tell me. Let me guess the rest. The big payoff came—"

"The same day somebody shot K. D. Becker," Frank finished.

"That's more than suspicious coincidence," Joe said. "Do you think forty grand would be enough for him to put a bullet in a friend? Don't forget, he has an alibi."

"We'll work on the alibi later," Frank said. "As for the money, it's not exactly chump change, and it might be only a partial payment, anyway. Whoever hired him might be holding out the rest until Oberman finishes the job."

"I thought you said all his debts were paid off," Joe said.

"He probably has other, hidden debts that a routine credit check wouldn't uncover," Frank reasoned. "I didn't have enough time to do a complete rundown."

"Sorry," Joe replied, patting his pile of books. "They didn't have any more detective novels at the library."

"It doesn't matter," Frank told him. "Even the most detailed credit history wouldn't tell us what we really need to know."

Joe looked at his brother. "What's that?"

"Who hired him," Frank said pensively. "Unless Oberman's a professional hit man—which I doubt—whoever hired him would have to be someone who wanted Becker dead and also knew about Oberman's money problems."

"Look on the bright side," Joe responded. "That should narrow down the list of suspects."

Frank gazed out the window. The sun warmed the inside of the car in defiance of the bitter cold on the other side of the thin glass. "I still think Crawford's behind the whole thing."

He twisted the key in the ignition and started the car. "If we don't crack this case in the next twenty-four hours, we never will. We should get home tomorrow night."

"Maybe if we shake things hard enough, the case will break wide open," Joe replied.

Frank nodded. "That's exactly what I was thinking."

"So where do we start?"

"With the sheriff," Frank said as he drove away from the library.

Joe appeared doubtful. "Can we trust him?"

"We have to," Frank answered. "We don't have much choice. Becker's life is still in danger since Oberman has to finish his job. If our theory's right, he'll definitely try again. K.D. needs police protection right now.

"And if I'm wrong about Stevens," he added, "telling him what we've uncovered will definitely shake things up."

Chapter 16

THE HARDYS almost had a head-on collision with the sheriff's jeep when they drove into the small parking lot on the side of the police station. Both cars screeched to a halt, close enough to rub fenders.

The horn on the jeep blared, and the siren whooped. Frank shifted their car into reverse and started to back up.

Joe suddenly shoved his door open, bolted out, and vaulted across the hood. He rushed over to the jeep, jerked open the passenger-side door, and jumped in.

He gave the sheriff a wide, warm smile. "Hi. Where we going?"

The sheriff's face turned an angry red as he glared at Joe. "You've got exactly five seconds to get out of this vehicle," he growled.

"Arrest me if you want," Joe said. "But if you're in a hurry to get someplace, you'll still have to take me with you. Just listen to what I have to say while you're driving, and you can throw me in jail later."

The sheriff scowled out the windshield as Frank pulled his car out of the way. "I suppose the two of you are a package deal."

Joe nodded. "That's right. A matched set. Two for the price of one. What do you say?"

The sheriff's gaze lingered on Joe for a long, silent second. Then he sighed, rolled down his window, and stuck his head out. "Hurry up and get your carcass over here!" he shouted in Frank's direction. "You're holding up police business!"

"So where are we going?" Joe asked again as they blasted down the highway with the siren wailing and the lights flashing.

"There's a state police roadblock up ahead," the sheriff answered. "I had my deputies stake out the garage in town where Gentry stores his truck. I figured he'd need his truck if he wanted to get very far.

"It didn't work out quite the way I planned. Gentry did go for his truck and he also got one of my men.

"The state troopers stopped them at the roadblock," he continued. "What we have now is what you might call a Mexican standoff. Gentry won't let Harlan go, and we can't let Gentry go."

"Gentry's bluffing," Frank said confidently. "He won't hurt your deputy. You know he's not the shooter."

The sheriff snorted. "Still think it's Pearson and Crawford?"

"They're involved," Frank replied. "But I don't think Pearson shot K. D. Becker anymore." He quickly told the sheriff what they'd discovered about Dick Oberman's debts and Walt Crawford's grazing rights. "The only thing missing," he concluded, "is a link between the two."

The sheriff didn't respond right away. Frank couldn't tell if he was lost in thought or just concentrating on the road. When he finally spoke, it was in a heavy voice with a touch of sadness. "I wish I could say there isn't a link. But there is one.

"Walt Crawford owns a lot of buildings in town," he explained. "Oberman's store is in one of them."

"So if Oberman fell behind in his rent," Joe ventured, "Crawford would know he had money trouble."

The sheriff's revelation set off a chain reaction in Frank's head. "I'll bet Crawford also owns the garage where Gentry stores his truck."

"You'd win that bet," the sheriff responded as he hit the brakes and the jeep skidded to a halt at the roadblock.

The state police had Gentry boxed in. Two patrol cars blocked the road ahead, and two more had moved up from behind. Eight uniformed troopers crouched behind the hoods and trunks. Sixteen eyes, three shotguns, and five revolvers were trained on the pickup truck.

"Put those weapons away before somebody gets hurt!" Sheriff Stevens bellowed as he lumbered out of the jeep.

A jittery trooper whirled around, his service revolver gripped tightly in his hand.

The sheriff put his hands on his hips and gazed evenly at the young officer. "Don't point that thing at me, son."

The trooper wavered for a moment and then holstered the gun.

The sheriff smiled softly. "That's more like it. Now let's see if we can undo whatever damage has been done here." He strode past the state police cars and approached the pickup truck. "Gentry!" he called out. "There's a couple of young fellows here who say you've been framed, and they've pretty much convinced me they might be right. If you surrender now, you may end up a free man. That's your best choice. I'd take it if I were you. Otherwise, you'll find yourself on a mighty hard road."

A few hours later Frank and Joe were back at the Elk Springs Police Station, sitting around a table with the cowboy sheriff and the Native American activist.

"You understand we're going to have to hold

you until we get this business cleared up?" the sheriff said.

Gentry nodded. "I only ask to be treated fairly, like anybody else. I trust Frank and Joe. If you're working together, I think I can trust you too."

The sheriff glanced over at Frank. "I can't say I like this idea much. Walt and I go back a long way. I'd rather confront him outright and see what he has to say."

"If you really thought that was a better idea," Frank countered, "you'd be doing it now instead of sitting here with us. You know we don't have any proof that Crawford was involved."

"We don't even have any hard evidence that Oberman pulled the trigger," Joe added. "If we can't shake his alibi, we have to force his hand somehow, get him to incriminate himself."

"And that's what this plan is all about," Frank said.

"I still don't like it," the sheriff muttered through his mustache. "I was hoping I could get some information out of Pearson, but I just wasted an hour at the hospital talking to myself. He's playing deaf, dumb, and blind. He didn't see anything, he didn't hear anything, he's tired and he needs to rest, and he's not going to answer any questions without a lawyer."

"He's either too scared to talk," Joe ventured, "or he's still hoping to use whatever he has to blackmail Crawford."

The sheriff put his hands on the table and pushed himself out of his chair. "All right. Let's do it before I change my mind." He checked his watch. "It's five-thirty now. Oberman's store closes at six."

"Then we'd better get moving," Frank said.

Oberman was alone in the store when the Hardys walked in. He greeted them with a smile. "I was just about to close. I can stay open for a little while if there's something you need, but I want to get over to the hospital to see K.D. before dinner."

"Then you haven't heard the news," Frank said gravely.

Oberman lost his smile. "What news?"

"She seemed just fine," Frank began in a faltering voice. "We were sitting in her room, talking. A nurse came in and gave her some kind of shot. She must have had an allergic reaction."

"What do you mean?" Oberman asked. "What happened? Is she all right?"

"I don't know," Frank said. "She started having trouble breathing. Then all of a sudden she passed out. Joe ran out to get a doctor. An emergency team swarmed into the room. They wouldn't let us stay while they worked on her. When they came out, all they'd say was that she was resting."

"I hope she'll be all right tomorrow morning," Joe said. "She sort of left us on the edge of our seats. She was telling us about what happened the morning she was shot."

Oberman's eyes locked on him. "What did she say?" he snapped. "Did she see anything?"

Joe shrugged his shoulders. "The conversation never got that far."

Frank glanced down at his watch. "We're running late. We were supposed to be at the sheriff's office ten minutes ago."

Oberman's cold blue eyes darted between the two brothers. "Why does the sheriff want to see you?"

"I'm not sure," Frank answered. "Something about what time it was when we found K.D. the morning she was shot."

Joe tugged on his brother's arm. "We really should get going." He gave Oberman a parting smile. "Maybe we'll see you again before we leave town."

The trap was set, and the bait was in place. Now all they could do was wait to see if Oberman would bite.

Peering down at the luminous dial on his watch, Frank realized he must have nodded out for a while. The last time he'd checked, it was a little after midnight. Now it was one-fifteen. He couldn't imagine how he had managed to fall asleep on the cramped, hard floor of the closet, and he hoped it wouldn't happen again. He had to stay awake all night if necessary.

The closet door was open just enough for Frank to have a view of the door into the dark room and the lumpy form on Becker's hospital bed. After a few minutes of staring into the gloom, Frank's eyelids started to droop again.

They did pop open, though, when a thin shaft of light leaked in from the hallway. A shadowy figure slipped silently into the room and padded quietly across the floor to hover over the bed for a moment. Then the person picked up a pillow and brought it down over the patient's face, pressing down firmly with both hands.

The patient thrashed around for a few seconds as the intruder pushed down harder. The thrashing grew weaker and weaker and finally died out.

Chapter 17

THE INTRUDER leaned over the still body on the bed. Frank burst out of the closet and lunged at him. Somebody hit the light switch and the room was flooded with harsh, fluorescent light.

Dick Oberman whirled around with the pillow still clutched in his hands. He threw it at Frank and whipped a hunting knife out of his jacket. He slashed wildly, half-blinded by the sudden glare. Frank jumped back, and the ugly, curved blade sliced through the air, inches from his chest. Oberman raised the knife over his head.

The body on the bed lurched up and grabbed the knife-wielding arm. Oberman's face twisted into a contorted grimace. Frank didn't know if it was caused by the shock of the dead coming back to life or the pain of the bone-crushing grip on his wrist.

Oberman howled and the knife clattered to the floor. Joe jumped off the bed, still clutching Oberman's wrist, and twisted the man's arm behind his back.

Frank smiled at his brother. "You've got fast reflexes for a corpse."

Joe grinned back. "Being dead isn't as bad as I thought it would be. In fact, it's a lot like my former life."

Frank looked over at Sheriff Stevens, who was leaning casually against the wall next to the light switch. "Think you can make a case now?" Frank asked.

The sheriff pushed up the brim of his cowboy hat and nodded silently.

"This is all a horrible mistake," Oberman protested.

"That's right," the sheriff drawled. "And you're the one who made it.

"There's only one thing I can't figure," he continued. "I talked to one of the waitresses at the diner across the street from your store. She claims she saw you changing the display in the front window around eleven o'clock on the morning K.D. was shot. But I don't see how that's possible."

"That's because you believed the watch," Frank answered. "Since K.D.'s broken watch said ten forty-six, everybody assumed that was the time of the shooting. But K.D. can't remember doing anything for over an hour and a half before that."

"That doesn't mean anything," Oberman objected. "The doctor said—"

"Why don't you just shut your mouth and listen politely?" the sheriff suggested forcefully. "Even if I can't prove you tried to kill K.D. the first time, I caught you in the act this time." His eyes shifted to Frank. "But I'm still curious."

"It's really pretty simple," Frank said. "He shot her between nine and nine-fifteen. When the snow let up for that short period, he was able to see. He smashed her watch then and moved the hands ahead to ten forty-six. Only a professional skier like Oberman could make it back to town by eleven. None of the rest of us could, but obviously he did. Also, he'd know any shortcuts through the mountains. The storm didn't stop completely until about ten, so the new snow covered his tracks near the crime scene. That's what was bothering me earlier. K.D. had some snow on her, so she couldn't have been shot at ten forty-six. The snow had stopped falling by then."

"Hold on a minute," the sheriff said. "This makes sense so far, but don't you think Oberman would have noticed that Becker was still alive when he came down into the canyon to break the watch?"

"Probably," Frank said. "But what could he do about it then? He wanted to make the shooting look like an accident. If he shot her twice, nobody would swallow the accident theory. Framing Gentry with the anonymous phone call and planting the rifle was an afterthought."

"How did you figure out that the watch was smashed deliberately?" Stevens asked.

"Actually," Frank replied, "I'm surprised none of us thought of it before. The watch was under her padded glove, and she fell in a pile of soft, new-fallen snow. Under those conditions, an accidental break would have been a million-to-one shot."

"Well, I've certainly learned a lesson from all this," Joe responded. "From now on, I'm strictly a digital watch man."

The Hardys managed to get a few hours' sleep in what was left of the night after the sheriff hauled Oberman off to jail. Before the long drive back to Denver in the morning, they stopped at the hospital to say goodbye to K.D.

"So you saved my life again," she said. "It's hard to believe that Dick Oberman tried to kill me. I'm kind of confused by it all. Why did you want to know if he could build a radio transmitter? And how was Mark Pearson involved in the whole thing?"

"It's all connected," Frank told her. "Pearson saw two people near the canyon that morning when he was tracking cougars. He saw Ted Gentry, and he also saw Dick Oberman. He tried to blackmail Oberman. Oberman told Crawford, and Crawford decided to eliminate Pearson."

"So Crawford lured him up to the cliff," Joe continued, picking up the story. "And while Crawford distracted Pearson, Oberman cut the brake lines on Pearson's truck."

Becker still looked confused. "But what does any of that have to do with my radio telemetry gear?"

Frank grinned. "That's the best part. Oberman had no way of knowing where you'd be. So he rigged up a radio transmitter to lure you to him. He wanted you to think a cat had entered that area. He probably planned to get rid of the transmitter after he shot you. Either he couldn't find it in the snow, or he forgot about it. Discovering you were still alive must have rattled him badly. Oberman's used to shooting at targets with a small-caliber weapon, not hitting live victims."

"Right," Joe said. "You're not dead because Oberman wasn't familiar with hunting rifles. He didn't consider the stopping power of the gun at long range. He figured all he had to do was hit the target."

"It sounds pretty complicated," Becker said. "How can you prove that Walt Crawford was behind Oberman?"

Frank chuckled. "We don't have to. Oberman hasn't stopped talking since he was arrested."

"Looks like your cats will be safe now," a deep voice commented from behind them. Frank turned and saw Ted Gentry standing in the doorway.

Becker smiled. "They're not *my* cats. They don't belong to anybody. They're wild and free. That's the way it's supposed to be."

"It sounds like a good life to me," Gentry replied.

"It sounds like a great first verse for a hit single," Joe ventured. "Let's get a camera and make a music video."

Frank shot a look at his brother. "Let's go home instead. I think you need a rest from your vacation."

Frank and Joe's next case:

Crosscut, Oregon, is a town divided. Two rival lumber mills are in fierce competition, while the tension between pro- and anti-logging forces threatens to tear Crosscut apart. And when an explosion at one mill claims the life of its owner, the police charge Callie Shaw's uncle, environmentalist Stan Shaw, with the murder!

Frank and Joe refuse to let Stan take the fall. But the land around Crosscut is rough country—and the men in it are even rougher. Before the boys can clear Stan's name, they'll have to clear a path through a dangerous world of chain saws and bulldozers, dynamite and double-barreled shotguns . . . in *Deadfall*, Case #60 in The Hardy Boys Casefiles™.